I0718715

BLEEDING SOULS SAVED BY LOVE

Warts an' All

Manda Mellett

COPYRIGHT

Warts an' All – Bleeding Souls, Saved by Love Series

Copyright © 2021 by Manda Mellett

ISBN: 978-1-912288-98-4

All rights reserved. No part of this book may be used or reproduced in any manner whatsoever including but not limited to being stored in a retrieval system or transmitted in any form or by any means, electronic, mechanical, photocopying, recording or otherwise, without the written permission of the author.

This book is a work of fiction. Names, characters, businesses, organizations, places, events and incidents either are the product of the author's imagination or are used fictitiously. Any resemblance to actual persons, living or dead, events, or locales is entirely coincidental.

WARNING : This book contains sexual situations, violence and other adult themes. Recommended for 18 and above.

CONTRIBUTOR PAGE

Cover Design by Jess FX

Edited and formatted by Maggie Kern @ Ms.Kedits

Proof reading by Darlene Tallman

CHAPTER 1

TOAD

What the fuck is she doing?

While watching the mad woman ahead I remain seated on my bike brushing sand off the tank—left courtesy of the recent sandstorm—before it gets the chance to turn into mud. Heavy raindrops are starting to fall, bouncing off my wet-weather gear that I'd put on earlier when I stopped, and already lightning flashes and thunder rolls overhead. Unlike the target of my scrutiny, I know a thing or two about Arizona weather.

Has she got a death wish or something?

She has just gotten out of her smart-looking convertible and has rushed over to the wash that's spilling over the road enough so it's stopped traffic. She's frantically yelling something and waving her arms. *Oh, fuck no.* I tense as I watch her climb down the bank.

Now Arizona hasn't got a stupid drivers' law for nothing, and most people, *except her,* seem to have their heads screwed on right, and have stopped, bunkered down in their cars as water floods the road, or, like me, are patiently sitting on their bikes.

Not that there are any more like me. I'm riding solo today and just didn't make it back in time. Still, it's Arizona in the summer, and much of what I expect. Hence, I never ride anywhere without my rain clothes in my saddlebags.

With a quirk to my lips, I continue to watch the free entertainment. The girl's getting drenched. Her tight designer t-shirt is clinging to her in such a way I wish she'd turn around, ready to award her plus points if she's not wearing a bra. Mmm mmm. *Come on, baby, give me a show.* Those tight shorts of hers hug a shapely ass. Ain't doing me no bother sitting here watching the scenery for a while, just like every other fucker—though they're nice and dry cocooned in their cars.

Hot damn it. She's just slipped. That water's not to be reckoned with. If she goes under, she'll have a hard time getting back up. It might confuse some folks who think of Arizona as a desert, that you can drown in one of our monsoons. Especially if you lose your footing and knock your head on the concrete.

Glancing around, I see all eyes on her, but nobody moves. Shit and damnation, I can't just sit here. I've got to do something. Telling myself at least I can't get any wetter, I kick down the stand and hoist my leg over the bike. Then I saunter on down, getting close enough so I can make myself heard over the roar of the rain which is coming down in sheets now, and the almost constant grumbles of thunder.

"What the fuck do you think you're doing?" I grab at her arm to steady her, as my voice has made her jump and lose her balance. "Easy, Princess. I got you." The mud's getting more slippery by the second. I decide to remove us from the danger before we both slide down. Mud wrestling wasn't on today's agenda, much as with the likes of her, it would probably be fun.

"Let me go!" Her voice is indignant as her hands bat at my arm, trying to escape my hold. When I don't let go, she adds, "If you're here, then help me."

"Sure I'll help, Princess. I'll help you back to your car." If I don't sound patient, it's no fucking wonder.

"No!" Surprising me with her strength, she pulls her arms away. "I can't leave her."

"Her?" Anxiously, I peer around the woman, trying to see who she's talking about. The urgency in her voice gets to me, especially as I recognise it's tinged with terror.

"Who's here? Where are they?" Peering forward, I acknowledge I'm no white knight, but the thought of someone—maybe a kid?—being in danger gets me moving further down into the wash. If they're as slight as the little thing who's standing next to me, they'll be no match for the strength of the waters which are rising by the second.

"It's Rolo," she cries frantically.

"Rolo?" What the fuck name is that for anyone? I've heard some bad monikers in my time, own one of them myself. But… *Rolo?*

"My dog. She jumped out of the car. The thunder frightened her, and I had my windows down because the air-conditioning's stopped working. It wasn't raining so hard then, but she just panicked and took off—"

"You're putting your life in danger because of some fuckin' dog?" Again, I make a grab for her, and this time I take a firmer hold. "Look, lady, I don't know what you think your game is, but the water's rising fast, and it's fuckin' suicide for you to be down here."

"I can't leave her."

Jesus Christ! The stubborn little thing's struggling to push me away and I'm all too conscious we've got an audience. I'm wearing my cut, the one that announces to all and sundry that I'm a member of the Wicked Warriors MC—outlaws in the eyes of the authorities. One phone call that I'm molesting a girl in full view will surely bring the cops. And with my luck, a patrol car will be stuck this side of the wash.

My options, I sum up quickly, are either to leave her or to go look for her fucking dog. If it was just her, I'd not have much conscience about leaving her to her own devices and hoping someone else would be crazy enough to stop her drowning. But as it happens, I'm a sucker for canines. Poor thing's probably scared out of its wits, and it's already disadvantaged by having her as an owner.

"Which way did it go?" I shield my eyes, not from the sun, which won't yet be making an appearance, but to ward off the blinding raindrops dripping off my hair and into my eyes.

Pointing, she cries, "She ran that way."

Up into the wash. Of course she fucking did. Thankful my motorbike boots will at least keep my feet dry, but already mentally lining up the services of a prospect to clean them off when I get back to the club—unless this princess offers to do the job herself, which I think is highly unlikely—I take a step, then pause.

"What's my reward to be, Princess?"

"What?" Crazed eyes find mine. *"Reward?"*

I shrug. "You're asking me to do a job. Don't you normally pay for a service?" Or looking at her, maybe she doesn't. That car of hers must have cost a fucking fortune. Probably given to her by her daddy.

"Oh, you want money." She rolls her eyes. "I've got money. I'll pay you. Just find my dog."

"Nah. I don't need your money." I view her again. In our short altercation, I've picked up she's spoilt and expects everyone to dance to her tune. I don't need more dollars. I've plenty enough for what I need out of life, but I want her to pay something for putting me out. "Dinner and a kiss will do for a start."

"Dinner?" Her voice has risen as though I'm speaking a foreign language. "You want me to go out for a meal with you?" That she says it in a way that suggests she could imagine no greater punishment spurs me on to rub salt into the wound.

"No, Princess. You're asking for my labour. I want yours. I find your dog, you cook me dinner at your house."

"I cook…" She can't even finish the sentence. She looks so shocked I want to laugh. But her nervous glances at the rising water that's so loud it's making it hard to hear must influence her. "Okay. I'll cook you dinner."

"Gonna hold you to that, Princess."

A fool could see time's running out. For now, I take her word for it, not having the least doubt she'll try and retract any invitation later, and set off upstream. The current's so strong it's already threatening to knock me off my feet, and I'm no lightweight. Leaning into the flow, I continue on.

It's no use me calling. My voice would be lost in the rush of the torrent, but I do have an advantage. While we'd been negotiating terms for the rescue, I'd seen a flash of something on the edge of the bank. That's now where I head for.

I should have asked her what kind of dog I'm looking for, but I'm sure I saw a tail poking out. I stride on, heading in that direction, then inwardly curse as I see what I thought was part of a retriever is nothing of the sort. Damn, it's just a bit of material that got caught on a twig.

Or is it? I'm about to move past when I look down again. *Is that…?* Nah, it's a rat, something I'm not going to rescue. *Hold on.* I back up, bend down, reach out my hand and ease a clump of vegetation back. Hell, there is an animal caught there—a creature with big eyes and one which has been trapped by branches being washed down by the water. For now, it's holding its head up, but won't last long.

I don't want a fucking rat bite. But somehow, I can't move on. *Fuck it.*

I'm an outlaw biker. I've killed men with my bare hands, but I can't let an innocent creature suffer. Parting the debris, almost blinded by the rain, I free the creature. Then, blinking hard, grab at it.

I get a nip on my fingers, but hell, this bedraggled thing is no rat. Though its features are all in miniature, it's definitely a canine, but barely larger than my hand.

A fucking handbag dog. A chihuahua. I frown as I pick it up and hold it close. As though now sensing a friend and safety, the mouth opens, and a tongue comes out and licks me. It's fucking tiny.

One of my friends runs a dog rescue and I've spent many a night sharing a drink and listening to how he'd put the world to rights. One way is to murder all fucking dog breeders who, instead of breeding for health, breed to order.

What was the word he used? Teacup dogs. Tiny versions, or what he'd call the runt of the litter, sold for thousands.

Trust Princess to go for one she could show off, without giving a damn about the health problems that could assail it.

I slip it under my waterproof jacket and, with not a little difficulty, get myself up the bank. As I do, I notice the sticks that had trapped it are suddenly swept away. Closing my eyes, I realise what a close call that had been. A few seconds later and the dog would have drowned.

As I walk back down toward the road, I notice she, too, has had the sense to get clear of the rushing water. When I near her, her face falls.

"You didn't find her." It might be drops of rain, but I swear she's crying.

In answer, I open my jacket to let her view the prize I'm carrying.

Her mouth opens in disbelief. "You got her? Oh my God. I thought I'd lost her." She holds out her hands. When I place the tiny chihuahua into them, she hugs it close, raining down kisses on its wet fur.

"Let's get you back to your car." I put my arm around her and help as she slips and slides in those designer shoes, which really are not up to this job.

When we reach her vehicle, I open the door for her, unable to be anything but amused to see rain has poured through the open windows and the leather seats have puddles on them.

"Put your windows up," I instruct. Heat won't be a problem until the rain stops. The temperature can drop forty degrees when we get one of the storms.

She obeys me, and I realise she can't get the windows up fast enough. Not just to keep her precious dog safe, but to cut me off.

Knowing electric windows stop when they feel pressure, I place my palm against the edge of the rising glass.

"Aren't you forgetting something?"

She switches her attention from the dog she can't stop fussing over, and her brow creases when she looks up at me. For a second, it looks like she's trying to find the answer, then her features relax. "Er, thank you?"

I wave her insincere gratitude off. "Your number, Princess. So I can call you and arrange to come over. I'm a meat man, by the way." I wink. "I'm not into vegetables."

Her mouth opens and shuts, her eyes narrow, her jaw clenches, then the tension again eases away. "My number, yes." She rattles off the digits fast, probably expecting I won't remember. But I've got a good head for numbers, and I know I won't forget.

"I'll call you," I tell her.

"Do that."

Immediately, I step away and she wastes no time closing the window. If I'm not mistaken, that was the locking of the doors that I heard.

My lips curve and I'm tunelessly whistling as I walk back to my bike. Swinging my leg over the saddle, I settle down to wait the weather out.

I grin to myself. That was my good deed for the day, and I'll hopefully get a nice steak dinner out of it.

Do I trust she gave me the right number? Fuck no. I'm not stupid. She wouldn't do that.

She also doesn't have a clue who she's dealing with.

I'm Toad. I'm the prez of the Wicked Warriors MC. Arizona chapter. My princess will be seeing me a lot sooner than she expects.

CHAPTER 2

RUBY

From the time Rolo jumped out of the car to her being back here safely beside me took little more than ten minutes, but must have taken years off my life. Such as Arizona summer monsoons are wont to do, they come down hard and fast, then ease, then the sun comes back out, making you wonder what all the fuss was about.

As the waters start to ease, cars around me start their engines. After another minute, the first couple start to ease their way across. Water sloshes from their tyres, cascading over their roofs, but it's no longer high enough to force them to stop.

Likewise, I press the ignition, noticing my hands are still shaking.

"You scared me half to death, Rolo."

Flicking a look down at where she's still curled up in my lap, shivering. I hope my body heat will be enough to warm her. She's such a small little thing. Apart from the cold, she must have been terrified half to death. Thank heavens someone came to help me. Though at the time, I don't know which I was most frightened of, losing my dog, or the man who came to my aid. *He was scary.* But he'd got her back. Something I'm not sure I could have done by myself.

Damn the air conditioner failing. My car's almost new. It shouldn't have such a fault. I'll get Daddy to return it to the shop. I'd had no choice but to wind down the windows. Who wouldn't, in one-hundred-degree heat? I never thought about Rolo jumping out. Never expected her to, but that crack of thunder had been particularly loud. As a dog mom, I feel a failure. She's already been through so much in her short life.

As the sun bakes down, heating the car, I'm sweating

profusely by the time I arrive home. Pausing, I wait for the automatic gates to slide open, knowing I have to leave enough time for whichever guard is on duty this afternoon to check who I am. I slide my hand over Rolo's body. Her shivering has stopped now, and her fur is almost dry.

The gate, at last, opens, and I drive down the driveway, sweeping around in a loop to park outside the garage. As I get out, holding Rolo to me, I shake my head as I look up at the sky. Not a cloud to be seen and the sun shining brightly. If I hadn't lived in Arizona all my life and knew only too well what to expect, I'd have thought my recent nightmare had been in my imagination.

As I approach the front door and step inside, I put Rolo down. Buster, the massive Rottweiler, comes rushing over.

Well, I grin to myself, *Rolo's certainly got her spirit back.* She's standing in front of me, barking and growling, when Buster tries to get close to me.

"Hey, monster." Bending down, I hold her back, while giving Buster a good rub behind his ears. She's a recent addition and hence the interloper. No one's told her she's a fraction of his weight, and bless him, the much larger dog lets her get away with murder. "You're totally spoilt," I tell the chihuahua who was responsible for all my troubles earlier.

"You look awful." My father appears from his study.

I throw my car keys toward him. Showing his reactions are sharp, he catches them in one hand. "My freaking air conditioner stopped working. I had to drive with the windows down through the rain." It's on the tip of my tongue to tell him exactly what happened, but I decide to hold back. The biker's rescue of Rolo wasn't important. Well, it was to the extent it got her back, but apart from that, not worth mentioning. I've already mostly forgotten him.

Daddy's eyes widen. "I'll get Parker to take it into the shop. You've only had it six months."

I shrug. It's not like I did anything to sabotage it. I just get in and drive.

"Sir? There's a phone call for you." Masters approaches, holding out a phone.

Daddy takes it, grins, then reverses his tracks back the way he has come, his mind clearly on other matters now. "You got it sorted?" The question is not for me, but for his butler-come-right-hand man.

As his voice trails off, I pick up Rolo once again, then proceed up the stairs to my bedroom. Inside, I place her on the floor, then shimmy out of my ruined clothes, leaving a trail of them behind me as I go to the bathroom.

I used to watch programmes about various stars' cribs on television, always comparing them to my own. Okay, so the mansion doesn't belong to me, but this here is my domain, and it puts many other bedrooms I've seen to shame. My shower is enormous—multiple rainfall heads and jets that would be the envy of even some of the superstars. I've a huge tub too, great for soaking after a day of not doing very much at all.

Before starting the shower, I make sure the towel that the maid left warming for me is positioned within reach as soon as I get out. Then I stare at my naked body for a moment.

My boobs could do with being a little larger, but as for the rest of me, I keep myself in shape. Which isn't a surprise. With a basement equipped with all the gym equipment I could ask for, and a personal coach who comes in three days a week, I should be in top form.

The chef, well, he makes sure my food is both nutritious and tasty, keeping an eye on the sugars and fats, so I don't need to do it myself. My father, having lost his parents early, is a health fanatic, and a lot of that has rubbed off.

I shower, then dry off and wrap a towel around my wet hair. I consider calling Anya, the maid to come dry and style it for me, but decide for once, I'll do it myself. All I've got planned is dinner with my father, and tonight, there'll be no guests I'll need to impress.

Wrapping my robe around me, I go to my walk-in closet, which alone must be the size of some large apartments. The walls are lined by rack after rack of stylish designer clothes, most provided courtesy of my personal shopper. I take down a lightweight jumper, holding it against me, seeing how it shows off the blue of my eyes, then remove the tag in order to wear it. I pair that with capris and finally slip my feet into a pair of Louboutins. I might not be going out, but I've been programmed always to look the part. It pleases Daddy.

After I'm dressed, I sit to style my hair, staring into the mirror. My immaculate appearance contrasts with the memory of the biker in my head. I don't know what made me think of him, but for some reason, he comes to my mind. He's so far away from me in social station, it makes me grin as I remember what payment he thought he could expect. A meal at my table? One I've cooked myself?

I give an unladylike snort. I've never prepared my own food, not once, not ever. Even when I want a snack, if the chef's not there, the maid or Daddy's butler gets it for me instead.

I picture the biker sitting awkwardly at the dining table that can seat twenty, but which normally has just Daddy and me sitting at one end. Hell, but that man was ugly. Long rat-tailed hair being blown around his face, a jutting jaw, a nose that looked like it was at one time broken and not set properly, and a scar running down one side of his face. His bare arms had been covered with tattoos. The image of him sitting there, calmly talking to Daddy, has me giggling to myself.

Why should I reward him? The Brewsters were put on this planet to rule, and men like Rolo's rescuer there to serve us. That's the lesson that's been drilled into me all my life. *I owe him nothing.*

Placing a gold necklace around my neck and diamond studded earrings in my ears, I hear the dinner gong sounding.

Knowing how much Daddy hates me to be late, I hastily stand, grab Rolo, and carrying her once again, descend the stairs, noticing the mouth-watering aroma, tantalisingly growing as I approach the dining room.

Daddy is already seated, Masters waiting behind my chair. He pulls it out as I approach, then pushes it under me as I prepare to be seated. He flicks out the linen napkin and places it over my lap.

"Wine, Miss Brewster?" he asks politely.

I nod, then ask, "What's on the menu tonight?"

"Shrimp cocktail followed by lamb in tarragon."

Again, I incline my head. All will be tasty and low fat, and the portion size will be my exact calorie intake. Daddy will have larger portions, commensurate with his body weight.

"Are you ready for me to serve now, Sir?"

"Thank you, Masters. Yes."

At my father's permission, the butler walks away and starts lifting covers off the plates.

As Daddy asks about my day to make conversation, I settle into the easy familiarity of our dinnertime routine. This is all I've ever known—just me and Daddy, either eating alone, or at times with his business associates.

I've no siblings. My mom died having me. As I start to describe my mediocre day—without, of course, referring to the incident with the man so far beneath my station—I realise I want nothing to ever change. Or, perhaps, only so far as to exchange my daddy with a man who can similarly support me.

Who'd want responsibility or to have to work every day? I have everything I could wish for. I don't even need to ask for what I don't have. My needs are anticipated and my every desire is given to me.

I lower my hand under my chair, the shrimp I'm holding

between my fingers snapped up eagerly by an expectant Rolo sitting there.

I want for nothing, I remind myself.

So why is it sometimes I feel lonely? Why is there an ache. telling me there's something missing?

"How was your day, Daddy?" I shake off any feelings which affect my equanimity.

When he doesn't answer immediately, I glance my father's way, noticing that though he's as smartly dressed as usual, his face looks tired.

As my brow furrows, he seems to collect himself and answers, "A good day, baby girl. A very good day."

There's something about the way he says it that unsettles me, but I don't probe. I haven't been brought up that way. Women don't need to worry themselves about business—that's what he's always told me.

As soon as we place our cutlery down, Masters is there to clear our empty starter plates away. But before he can start serving the main dish, a loud bell sounds.

Daddy's eyebrows rise, and he tilts his head toward the butler. His expression suggests he wasn't expecting anyone.

"Excuse me, Sir, I'll just go and get that." Masters bends at the waist, then walks backward out.

Again, I glance at my father, but his brow is creased as his eyes are fixed to the door through which Masters disappeared, as if he has no idea who could have come calling.

We wait, empty placemats in front of us. My tummy rumbles, reminding me the low-calorie dressing and the shrimp themselves had only just whetted rather than satisfied my appetite. Fidgeting, I reach down with my hand to pet Rolo.

When the door reopens, expecting our dinner to be resumed, I breathe a sigh of relief. One that I immediately gulp back down.

Masters is standing with his face impassive. "Sir, this gentleman says he's been invited for dinner."

What? My disbelieving eyes can't take it in, and I immediately think the word gentleman is a bit of a stretch. *How the hell did he find me?* My jaw drops in horror, and my eyes shoot to my father, silently begging him to get me out of this. But if I'd expected to see him horrified at the sight of the man who's just walked in, I'm to be disappointed. Instead, he's staring at Rolo's rescuer with a mixture of pleasure and welcome.

My eyes widen as my father whips off his napkin, lays it on the table, stands and approaches the rough-looking biker. What's more, he's extending his hand to him.

"Toad. It's good to see you. To what do we owe this pleasure?" He pumps his hand up and down once, then lets it go.

Pleasure? I grit my teeth. I'd be happy if I'd never seen him again.

He looks so out of place—worn jeans, tight t-shirt, a leather vest that looks so out of place, worn proudly. He's just the type of man my father always advised me to steer clear of. *So why's he greeting him like a long-lost friend?*

Toad beams my way. If he notices the glare I'm directing toward him, he makes no sign. His grin broadens as he explains to Daddy, "Your daughter invited me."

Daddy's face goes blank for a moment, then he looks my way with his eyebrow raised quizzically. "I didn't know you two knew each other."

Toad chuckles. His voice seems to vibrate right through me. "We don't. Well, we didn't, not until today. Not until I rescued her dog from the flood waters. Princess there invited me to dinner as a thank you."

My eyes narrow. He'd invited himself as far as I can remember.

"You did? She did?" If Toad's words have unsettled my father, he shows no sign of it. "Then dinner you shall have. Masters? A fresh plate, please. And tell Chef to make extras."

Masters eyes Toad up and down as if assessing his weight, and then nods his head.

They're all treating this like a normal occurrence. Me, though, I've had enough. I stand, my napkin dropping from my lap to my feet.

"You!" I point my finger at the man who I now know is called Toad. *It suits him. He's so damn ugly.* "I didn't invite you to eat a meal with us."

"No, you didn't," he agrees. "You agreed you'd cook for me. But this way means you don't need to go to any trouble."

"Cook for you?" Daddy, *the traitor*, snorts. "Sit yourself down, Toad." He points to the empty chair that's beside him and opposite me.

"Daddy, no." I protest. "There's no reason for Toad to be here. I don't want to eat with him."

Daddy's eyes harden. "Is he lying to me, Ruby? Has he told me a pack of lies? You didn't mention it, so maybe he is. Tell me direct. Did he, or did he not, do you a favour today?"

My mouth works. *I could lie. Daddy would believe me. All it would take is to suggest Toad's making everything up.* But I've been brought up to be honest, so I simply reply, "He did." My words are quiet and mumbled.

"And," Daddy continues, his voice hardening, "did you agree to have dinner with him?"

My cheeks flush. My temper rises, but I swallow it down. I don't give in to emotion. That's not how I've been raised. But the words sound like they're dragged out of me. "I kind of did. But I never—"

"Then sit, Toad. It seems my daughter owes you an apology and her thanks for helping her today."

CHAPTER 3

TOAD

I t's hard not to laugh out loud at the expression on Princess's face. She's clearly discombobulated at the sight of me in the palace in which she lives, her sanctuary where she thought she was safe.

I'd known exactly who I was dealing with today. It hadn't taken me but a moment to clock those personal plates. It had been, however, my first time speaking to her and meeting her face-to-face. But yet, she was nothing I hadn't been led to expect.

A spoilt daddy's girl, born with a silver spoon in her mouth, and since then, having had everything handed to her on a plate. It was obvious she'd looked down on me, a biker, and nothing, except for the life of her pet, would have driven her to voluntarily talk to me. For my part, I didn't much want anything to do with someone like her.

But while our meeting today had been coincidence, her life and mine are set to become intertwined.

Little did she know that her existence was all smoke and mirrors, and that her perfect life wasn't what she thought it was. You see, you could call her father a business partner of the Wicked Warriors MC Arizona chapter.

"Sit," Brewster invites me.

I'm amused as the butler rushes over to pull out the chair as if I was incapable of seating myself. He even fixes a goddamn napkin over my lap. Seeing an opportunity to yank Princess's chain further, I take a corner of the napkin and tuck it into the neck of my t-shirt. Well, it will protect my cut from spillage. Catching her look of disgust, I raise an eyebrow toward her.

I know my manners, but it amuses me to let her think me uncouth.

If I've shocked Brewster, he, unlike his daughter, shows no sign of it. Instead, he makes conversation.

"So, Toad. Tell me what happened today?" he asks me, but his eyes land on his daughter, and his lips purse.

Using as few words as possible, I explain what went down. As I do, I feel something touch my leg. It's annoying, as though an insect's trying to get inside my boot. Reaching down to swipe it away, I find my fingers are being licked. It's tiny Rolo, as if she knows I'm talking about her. Grinning, I pluck her up in just one hand and settle her on my lap.

Brewster's expression firms, but he says nothing. Princess though, if looks could kill, I reckon I'd be dead. So I make the most of petting Rolo and telling her what a good girl she is. Of course, the tiny chihuahua loves this, and soon settles down to sleep.

"Sounds like you owe Toad more than just words and a meal, Ruby." Brewster's clearly not happy with his daughter. "You dote on that pooch. And if not for him, she wouldn't be here."

Princess folds her arms and pouts. "I was doing fine until he came along. I could have gotten her myself."

My lips curve upward and my brows rise. We both know she's lying.

"Nevertheless, he did help. Ah, thank you, Masters."

It's not often someone approaches me unawares, but the butler has managed it, magically appearing at my shoulder and putting down a loaded plate. Guests are served first, it seems. I notice I've some delicious looking lamb on my plate, but if you ask me, there's not a lot of it. Brewster gets a plate slightly smaller, and that given to Princess must hold only half of what's on mine, or even less. Masters then places serving dishes of vegetables on the table. With a wink at Princess, I refrain from touching the broccoli or carrots, and just load my plate with roast potatoes instead. Not that I've anything against vegetables, but going without was worth it, just to see the revulsion on her face.

I all but snort when I see her pointedly take a giant portion of both.

The lamb is good, I decide, after just one mouthful—tender and tangy with the smooth taste of vanilla tinged with liquorice. The potatoes are crisp and seasoned just right, and it's no hardship to empty my plate. What's harder is resisting lifting it up and licking the remaining juices off. For a moment I'm tempted, just to see what expression Princess would wear then, but I refrain. I do, however, sweep my finger through the remnants of sauce, and make a showing of sucking it clean.

She huffs loudly and averts her face.

Brewster, himself, so focused on eating, either ignores me or doesn't notice.

When we've finished, the butler clears the table, then places a heaped bowl of fruit in the centre of it. When Brewster gestures to it, I shake my head.

Princess, however, takes an apple and bites into it.

"Tempting, Princess," I tell her and wink.

She looks horrified, puts the apple back down on her plate, then lifts it again as if not wanting to waste it. Me? I'm wishing she'd gone for a banana instead.

Coffee, presented in tiny cups, has been served and drunk when Brewster speaks next. "So, Toad, can you spare me a few minutes?"

I make a point of taking out my phone and looking at it. "Yeah. I can talk for a few."

"Ruby, please excuse us." Brewster pushes his chair away from the table, gets to his feet and stands. "This way."

As I copy his actions, remembering just in time to place Rolo on the floor and taking the napkin out of my shirt and laying it down, I notice *this way* takes me around her side of the table.

As I follow her father, I lean down and whisper into her ear, "Somehow I think you're going to be tastier than that meal we've just had. Maybe soon we'll put that to the test."

Her gasp of shock makes me chuckle as I exit the room and into the man of the house's office.

Brewster goes to sit behind his desk, gesturing me to the chair in front. Instead, I remain standing, with my arms crossed over my chest.

He grimaces. "The cartel won't take no for an answer."

I'm not surprised. Brewster's made his fortune dishonestly, working with the cartel to transport guns across the US. We launder his ill-gotten gains through our businesses, in which he's supposed to invest. We get a cut, he gets clean money, and so the world turns.

His mouth twists. "Enrico wants Ruby. He says she's old enough now."

"He's been patient," is my only response.

Again, he grimaces. "He's been married three times in the interim. None of his wives were of a strong disposition, or so it would seem." He means, Enrico killed them. "He can't have her, Toad. I won't allow it."

Unfolding my arms, I now take the offered chair. Pulling out a pack of cigarettes, I take one and light it. He gives me a look of disgust, but nevertheless pulls out an ashtray and places it in front of me. I inhale deeply, trying not to cough. In truth, I don't smoke much, not so as it's become a habit. But it's a gesture to see how far I can push him. That he makes no protest is a sign it's a fair distance.

I tap off some of the glowing ash. "You should have thought of that before you signed her over."

"Fuck, Toad." He wipes his hand over his face. "She was a fuckin' baby. I didn't even want the kid. You know I lost her mother because of her?"

I do, yes. Though I wouldn't have put it that way. Princess's mom had died in childbirth. It wasn't anything Ruby had had control over. I also know that Brewster had adored his wife, not so much the baby, and definitely not when birthing her had come at such a cost.

At the time, he'd thought nothing of promising her to the cartel as a gesture that he was fully invested. The cartel, of course, then had a hold over one of their most important men in the US. But as Ruby had grown, something about her had enchanted him. Whether she'd grown to be a clone of her mother, or just because she was herself, he doted on her. When he thought of her married to a man with a dubious reputation and twice her age, he'd baulked.

"What do your lawyers say?" I raise my eyebrow.

"There's no way out of it." His lips purse.

Of course, the contract between them didn't actually use the words trading flesh. But Brewster stood to lose everything if he didn't comply with the request. I suppose it says something about the make of the man that his fortune isn't totally worth his daughter's distress.

Realising I've smoked most of my cigarette, I stub it out in the ashtray he'd provided. "There is a way out of it. Ruby can't be married if she's already wed."

Brewster shakes his head. "Enrico knows that's an option. He doesn't mind marrying a widow."

Yeah, that's the threat. Anyone stupid enough to take Ruby as his wife will almost certainly soon end up dead. So who would be mad enough to do it? Only a man who daily stares death in his face and trusts the Devil to take care of him. Only a man with a ton of trusted protection at his back.

"Four million," I tell him.

His eyes find mine and narrow. "We agreed on two."

I shrug. "That was before I met Ruby today."

He appears to grit his teeth, and his jaw clenches. "I know she's not the easiest woman—"

I snort. *Easy?* Initiating her into MC life is going to be a trial and a test. A trial of my patience and a test of my strength. Of course, my VP, or any one of my brothers, might have stood up and taken a virgin princess, you know, take one for the team and all that. I had been considering that, before I'd realised she wasn't just some girl who'd just tell her daddy yes, and step into any role proposed to her.

I'd seen a backbone today. She's going to be quite the conquest. You know what though? I'm arrogant enough to think I'll have a chance of success. I'll have to. A quick divorce would just put her back in Enrico's sights. As for her being made a widow? He'd have to get through my club first.

Brewster sighs. "Have you any ideas how to play this? She doesn't seem to like you much."

"She doesn't like me at all," I tell him. And from what I've seen, I don't particularly care for her. She's spoilt, stuck up and a real bitch. There's nothing to warm me to her. Under normal circumstances, she's the last woman I'd take for my wife. But this isn't forever, just until we can get Enrico off our backs. Once he knows she's defiled, he'll go off the idea of her. Eventually. It might take her spitting out a couple of kids, but hopefully her lustre will lose its shine when she does.

I'm banking on the fact that taking an ex-prez's old lady is nothing like marrying a virgin princess. I'm signing up for years, maybe, but not forever. Just as long as I don't lose my life, or my sanity, in the process. And as I've otherwise no intention of taking any bitch as my own, it won't be too much of a hardship.

"Her meeting you today could be useful." Brewster taps his fingers against his desk. "Could put out the story. Biker rescues billionaire's daughter's pet. Could be the basis for a relationship that Enrico wouldn't question."

No, he'll just put a hit out on me. But to Brewster, I say, "That could work, yes."

He grimaces. "We're running out of time. Enrico's in the US."

"You think he's coming for her?" For myself, I'd say yes. He's been patient enough. She turned twenty-one a few months back, which was the age the contract had stipulated. Her father would have her for the first two decades and one year of her life. The leader of the cartel would have the rest.

His jaw goes tight. "I do."

I put my hand to my face, running my fingers along my bearded chin. Finally, I take a deep breath. "Then we've got to get her under the MC's protection. Sooner rather than later."

"But how?" Brewster asks. Then he shakes his head. "What does it matter? Kidnap her if you must, anything just to keep her safe. If she goes to Mexico…"

If she goes to Mexico, Enrico won't get the placid wife he expects. Instead, she'll be so unexpectedly spirited, his only option will be she'll be beaten into submission. Something I might need to do myself, but I'll be kinder about it. Some beatings she might even turn out to like. I can't hide my smile at the thought of it.

"Leave it to me." Placing both hands on the desk, I push myself to my feet. "I'll sort something out."

Brewster stands as well. "I don't care how the fuck you do it. But promise me this. She'll never know about the contract."

Well, hell. His instruction is nothing more than I expected, but how the fuck would it work? How do I convince my spoilt princess that I'm the man for her? Me, a jaded MC prez, fifteen years her senior. Me, a man I suspect that she hates.

Thing is, I've never yet run from a challenge. I don't intend to fail. Nor do I want to end up dead.

Well, no one said life was going to be easy.

CHAPTER 4

RUBY

"Good morning, Miss." Charity greets me as I enter the kitchen. "Your normal breakfast?"

Absently I nod as I go to get the bag of dog food out of the cupboard and fill a bowl for Rolo, who's dancing at my feet. Grinning, I place it down, realising I'm as much a servant to her, as my father's staff are to me.

"Your father ate earlier."

Not bothering to respond—it's normal for him to wake at dawn while I tend to sleep later—I take a seat at the wooden table in the middle of the room. "I'll eat in here," I tell her, not wanting the formality of the dining room.

Charity busies herself filling a bowl with fruit and placing it in front of me, along with a croissant, and follows it up with a pot of decaf coffee. She pours out a cup, then steps back to the worktop where she's got a newspaper spread out.

"Anything interesting?" I ask, reaching for an apple, before a vision of Toad's face appears in my head, making me change my mind and go for a pear instead.

"Not much. That damn motorcycle gang's in the news again."

That doesn't surprise me. "What have they done now?" Something, hopefully, to get Toad locked up so I never have to see him again. I'd noticed the Wicked Warriors emblem emblazoned on the back of his cut last night when he'd walked out with Daddy.

If there was ever a man I hated so much on sight, I can't remember having met him. I shudder as I eat my breakfast, wondering for the umpteenth time why my father had even let him into the house. He was uncouth, unkempt, rude and obnoxious. I could go on all morning, listing words to describe him, and none of them would be positive.

Charity's obviously skim reading. "A couple of the gang were arrested after a bar fight."

"When?" I innocently prompt. My hopes that Toad's now behind bars fades when she names an hour when I know he was still ensconced with my father—they'd spoken late into the night. Unable to sleep, I hadn't missed the roar of his motorcycle when he was leaving,

"Good morning, Miss Ruby." Masters comes in. He smiles warmly at Charity, then his face grows professional as he greets me. "What are your plans for today? Will you need the car?"

I don't have any plans. I've nothing to do, nowhere to be. "I'll drive myself if I go anywhere," I state, before remembering my air conditioner is broken. "On second thought, my car's out of action, so can you warn Henri I might be needing him?"

Masters raises an eyebrow. "Your car is fixed, Miss Ruby. It was returned first thing." *It was?* My father's normally slower getting around to anything. Masters rises and dips his chin. "The man who was here last night brought it back for you."

Now it's my turn to widen my eyes. *Toad?* Damn that man. I don't want to owe him anything. I put the last portion of pear into my mouth and feel like I'm biting down on cardboard. My stomach rolls, as I suspect Toad will want payment, and somehow, I don't envisage him accepting money.

I stand, leaving my plate to be cleared by Charity, well, that's her job, and calling Rolo, I step out of the kitchen. I'm only halfway to my room when my phone rings.

Taking it out of my pocket, I glance at who's ringing. *Unknown caller.* I debate about answering and come down on the side of ignoring it. I've only taken a few steps when my phone pings with a message coming in.

Unknown caller: Answer your phone, Ruby.

My eyes crease. A salesman wouldn't be so direct, would he? When the ringing tone starts again, I wonder if it's one of my friends who's got a new number.

"Ruby speaking," I answer, cautiously.

"Good morning, Princess."

Oh shit. It's him. "I have nothing to say to you."

There's a heavy sigh. "Just as I expected. Not even a fuckin' thank you. Or don't you know your car's back yet? I got it fixed."

I'm determined not to say thank you. That would imply that he's done me a favour. *Which he has.* Shrugging that thought away, I offer, "How much do I owe you?"

There's a snort on the line. "Oh, Princess, I don't want your money. Don't you know there are different ways to pay a man back?"

My stomach roils at the thought of what kind of payment a man like him could be expecting. "I didn't ask you to fix my car," I snarl. "So I don't owe you anything."

"Fact is, Princess, you might not have asked, but I've done it anyhow. I deserve lunch with you, at least, don't I?"

"I'm busy today."

"No, you're not."

"I am," I argue, knowing I'm sounding like a petulant child.

He chuckles, then sighs. "Have it your way, Princess." He ends the call abruptly.

I stand in the hallway, my mind in a mess. What is it about this man that gets me so worked up? I'm rich. I've had men chasing me before for all the wrong reasons, and I've had no problem before when I've turned them down. But Toad? I shudder. *What's he going to do next?*

I wonder about speaking to my father, but after his surprising display last night when he seemed to think I owed Toad for Rolo's rescue, I'm half convinced he'll persuade me to accommodate his wishes in regard to having my air conditioner repaired. After the reception Toad had gotten last night, nothing would surprise me. He might turn up unannounced and expect me to amuse him.

While I previously had no plans for the day, I hastily reconsider. If Toad's going to visit, I can't be in.

Reaching my room, I look into the mirror, then swap my casual jeans and t-shirt for a flowery summer dress. I find Louboutin shoes that match, and grab my Gucci handbag, then sort through Rolo's belongings for a harness that goes with my outfit.

What's a girl going to do when she needs to disappear? She goes shopping. Returning to the mirror, I grin at my reflection, then dressed in my rich-girl's armour, I pick up Rolo, go to the stairs and exit the house, pausing to pet Buster for a moment on my way out.

Blissful cool air starts flowing through my car only moments after I turn on the engine. Still, after her escapade yesterday, I make sure Rolo's firmly strapped in before proceeding down the driveway and out through the gates.

I don't *need* anything, but if spending my father's money was an Olympic sport, I could win a gold medal easily. Starting to look forward to my morning, I turn on the radio, tapping my fingers in time to the music. In a few moments, I start singing and even grin. If Toad has the audacity to turn up again, well, I won't be there waiting.

On the freeway, I put my foot down, enjoying the exhilaration of speeding. I don't worry about getting stopped by the cops, my father can buy my way out of anything. With reluctance, I start to slow as I reach the turnoff I should be taking, wondering for a moment whether to just keep driving. My indecision means I'm a second too late indicating.

Instead of forward progress, I feel something crashing into me which sends my car spinning. I scream, fight the wheel, and slam my foot on the brake, but I'm unable to do anything as the car lurches toward the edge of the road and dives into the ditch that runs alongside it, and begins rolling.

The sudden cessation of movement is startling, and I have to shake my head to clear it. My heart's beating too fast, and I'm fighting for breath in my panic. My chest hurts where the seatbelt tightened against it. My neck feels like I've wrenched it. *I'm upside down.*

Rolo.

Gingerly, aware I might have done myself some damage, I turn to check on her. She's whining, wriggling, hanging as she's still attached to her harness. I try to unbuckle my seatbelt to get to her, but it's stuck.

Is that smoke coming out of the engine?

My eyes look around wildly while I examine my predicament. There's another car up on the embankment. *Was that what hit me?* My mind's a blur, as I try to remember what caused the accident. *Me?* I left the turn late, I admit it, but I can't understand what happened.

I try the seatbelt again, needing to free myself, then bang on the window to attract attention. The other car's still on its wheels, so hopefully the driver won't be too badly injured.

I'm hyperventilating and know I'm panicking. I try to force myself to think straight.

My phone.

My Gucci bag might look impressive, but not from this angle, and not when it's out of my reach and there's no way to get it.

My car phone.

I'm disorientated but try to find the right button. But the ignition had cut out when the car had crashed and pressing it does nothing.

Blood rushes through my ears. *I need help. I need it now. That's smoke, I'm sure.*

I scream. Then scream again.

Suddenly, to my side, there's movement.

Oh, thank God.

Someone's wrenching my door open. Fresh air rushes in, as well as the sour smell of smoke, confirming my dire situation. My panic rises, but a hand reaches in and undoes my seatbelt. Arms support me as I drop, then I'm dragged from the car without a thought to any injury I might have, surely confirmation that the situation is urgent.

I bump onto the ground, my already dazed head spinning.

"Rolo!" I scream. "My dog!"

My rescuer doesn't speak to me.

I'm hurting, but I have to get to her. With one thought in mind, painfully, I roll onto my knees, then use my hands to push myself to my feet. I launch myself back to the car.

"Stupid bitch," an unknown voice snarls. "Get her in the car."

"My dog!" I struggle against the arms now holding me.

"Hurry it up," another voice says. "We need to be out of here."

I can't comprehend, can't compute what's happening. Instead of moving me a safe distance away and assessing my injuries, the man who extracted me from the wreckage is now dragging me. I stumble and am swept up into strong arms. As well as smoke, the odour of strong body sweat reaches me.

"Bring her," the second voice instructs again. "Before we get company."

What's going on?

Rolo's frantic yapping reaches my ears. "I need Rolo," I scream, more worried about her than what's happening to me.

The man ignores me and continues pulling me along and up the bank. It belatedly dawns on me this is no rescue and that quite possibly, this was no accident.

I start kicking, punching, but apart from a disgruntled oomph, it has no effect on him.

I hear cars on the highway rushing past. *Why is no one*

stopping? Why doesn't anyone come to see? But my car's out of sight, and it's possible no one saw what happened to me. All they'll see is what I'm looking at now—a car parked up on the shoulder with its hazard lights flashing.

Then, there's another sound—a roaring of motorcycle engines, but they'll just zoom past the broken-down vehicle like everyone else. I can't count on anyone to help me.

I fight. I give it all I've got. Now, I'm not just trying to get back to Rolo, but to save myself. My renewed effort causes the man to lose his hold on me, but the other sees what's happening and rushes back to help. The two overpower me easily. With my hands held firmly behind me, I'm pushed forward toward the open back door.

I dig in my heels. *This can't be happening.*

I've always known, of course, I'm a potential kidnap victim. My father's loaded. But stupidly, I never expected it to happen to me.

When I make one last futile attempt to avoid being pushed into the car, I'm punched in the face. It stuns me. I scream.

It's then, mayhem breaks out.

The sound of the motorcycle engines, which had become deafeningly loud, suddenly cease. Shots fire. I feel myself falling…

I must have blacked out. The next thing I know, I'm being driven at speed down the highway in the vehicle that must have run me off the road. There's a man in the front driving, and another in the passenger seat. I'm lying stretched out in the rear. My head throbs. Raising my hand, I touch my scalp, and it comes away red.

I feel dizzy, weak.

"Who are you? What do you want from me?"

The men say nothing, though the passenger turns his head and seems to look at me with sympathy before he looks back to the road again.

"I've got money," I cry out. "I can pay you. Just name your price. But take me back to get my dog."

There's no reaction. Painfully pulling myself into a sitting position, I reach for the door handle. We're going fast, but I'll do anything to get to Rolo. I'm probably not thinking straight, but I pull on the handle…

Child locks thwart me.

What the hell can I do?

"Please. I beg you. Take me back to my car."

There was smoke. My brain's working overtime—hearing Rolo's panicked yips and whines, seeing flames lap at her. *How can these men be so callous as to let her burn?*

"Talk to me!" I screech. "Who the hell are you?"

The car slows. *To turn around?* But we're turning in and driving through heavy metal gates, and along a track leading down to a large building.

There's a sign. I sit forward, brushing blood out of my eyes as I strain to read it.

Wicked Warriors MC. Arizona Chapter.

CHAPTER 5

TOAD

I stop my pacing as the medic appears. "What's the verdict?"

Scalpel throws his medical bag down and grins as he leans back against the wall. "Concussion, possibly. Metal said she hit her head hard on a rock when the goons let her go."

"She was bleeding." I state the obvious. My gut had rolled when I had seen the amount of blood on her. Her dress had been soaked in it. My anxiety level had shocked me, seeing she was supposed to be nothing to me but a job, a way to bring revenue into the club. I've seen women who've been hurt before, some knocked around by street punks, and once, we'd stumbled across a truckload of traumatised trafficked girls. While their plight didn't leave me completely cold, I hadn't become emotional and quickly focused on getting them the help that they needed. So why did the blood on Princess cause knots to form in my stomach?

"Of course she was fuckin' leaking the red stuff. Head wounds do that. I stitched it up." Scalpel shrugs. "Other injuries? Bruised ribs from the seatbelt, and a case of whiplash. Other than that, she got away lightly." He pauses, reaches into his pocket and takes out his cigarettes. After he lights up, he smirks. "She's cursing you up a storm."

I've no doubt she is. When I have a sudden yearning and gesture toward him, he offers me his pack. Christ, this woman's got me smoking more than I have for years.

Scalpel draws down smoke into his lungs and blows it out. "She's demanding to see you."

Yeah, again, I have no doubt on that matter. I resume the pacing that he'd interrupted, walking from one side of my office to the other. "She's advanced the fuckin' agenda," I tell him, half speaking to myself. "There's no way she can go home. Her father's security is shit." I pause to punch my fist against the wall. "What the hell was he thinking, letting her drive off alone?"

Scalpel allows a grin to form, and seeing it, I suspect it's at my expense. "I guess he finds it hard to control her, Prez." His unspoken suggestion is that I'm going to find the same. But my princess is soon going to learn, I'm a totally different animal to deal with than her doting dad.

I wave toward my phone lying on the desk. "I've just spoken to her father. He's upped the payment to five million."

Scalpel whistles and pretends to stagger. "I thought he'd already baulked at you doubling it last night?"

I shrug. "Seems today has focused his mind." If I hadn't placed that tracker on her car when we'd repaired the air conditioner, Enrico would have succeeded. By now, she'd be south of the border and possibly already wed.

"You keeping her here?"

I slam both my hands on my desk. "Got no other fuckin' option, have I? Enrico's putting pressure on Brewster, and he's going to fold. He's already running out of excuses."

Scalpel's grin widens further. "I think you're going to have to find a few of those yourself. She's itching to get out of here."

I bet she is. Half of me wishes I could keep her locked up and not have to deal with her, but leaving her to stew isn't an option. At some point, I've got to go through with the deal that I made with her father, and that means, I've got to get on her right side. Fuck knows how I'm going to do that.

I've only half smoked the cigarette, but I stub it out. Drawing a deep breath, I head toward the door. "Wish me luck," I toss over my shoulder.

He laughs and, "Good luck, Prez," follows me as I leave my office.

As I walk through the clubroom, there's no missing the smirk my VP, Raider, throws toward me. For a moment, I want to throttle him, but settle for raising my middle finger toward him instead. If it wasn't for the boost this would give to the club's coffers, I wouldn't even be considering taking on an old lady. But I'll play my part for the good of the club, even though I'd rather leave it to a prospect.

Outside the door of the room I'd told them to put Ruby in, I hesitate, wishing I believed in some deity that would give me the strength to do what I need to do next.

Taking a deep breath, I turn the key in the lock and walk in.

Ruby's lying on the bed, one arm flung up over her eyes. Her face is red and blotchy. When she registers someone's entering, she hastily sits up, then puts her hand to her forehead, reminding me she's in pain. If that hadn't been enough to tamp down my desire to read her the riot act for putting herself in danger today, her tears would probably have done it.

The sight of me, though, seems to make her steel herself. Although the effect is minimised by the arm hastily thrown over her chest to support her aching ribs, she pulls herself to her feet.

"You!" she hisses, her voice dripping with venom. "My father trusted you." I wait, knowing there's going to be more. "You ran my car off the road and kidnapped me."

Whoa. I should have been prepared for the conclusion she'd reached, but I hadn't. Tossing my hands into the air, I widen my eyes. "Me? Kidnap you? I fuckin' rescued you."

"And Rolo!" Ignoring me, her voice breaks. More tears fall and she can't hold back the sob as she wipes them away. "How could you just leave her there to die? To burn to death? I hate you!" She advances and when her hand rises, I grab hold of it just before it makes contact with my face.

"You've got it wrong," I tell her, capturing her other hand

when it goes for me too. "We weren't the ones to try to kidnap you. We rode in and saved the day."

"Sure." Her face reflects the sarcasm in her tone. "You'd love me to believe that, wouldn't you? My saviours in leather armour. You think my father won't see through your plot? How much are you going to ask him for in return for my release?"

My eyes roll. "Ruby, for fuck's sake, listen to me. I had nothing to do with causing you to run off the road."

She tries to pull back. I release her but stay wary in case she flies at me again. "Yeah." She scoffs. "You just happened to be there. Do you think I wouldn't recognise a setup when I saw one?" Again, the fire dies, as again she sobs, and I know she's thinking about that runt of a dog.

I know she's in pain, and mentally hurting, so I try to calm myself. Ruby is definitely difficult, but no one ever said she wasn't smart. However, in this case, two and two don't add up to anything more than four. The only explanation will have to be the truth. "I planted a tracker on your car when I fixed it earlier."

She'd turned her back on me, and now she swings around. Slowly she nods, then sneers. "I suppose that's exactly the kind of thing that you'd do. Just shows if you weren't responsible today, you would have been sooner or later." She moves stiffly, making allowance for her sore ribs, but still manages to take a stance with her hands on her hips. "So if not you, who were they? Who ran me off the road?"

Would it help her if she knew? I run my hands back through my hair and grimace. Knowing the cruel and elderly boss of a cartel is after you is probably too much to take. And, I'd promised her father.

"After last night, I wanted to see you again, Ruby." Truthfully, I'd rather have my teeth pulled at the dentist, but there are reasons why I have to lie. "You refused lunch. I was curious what pressing things you had to do. So yeah, I was tracking you." She was fucking lucky I was. "Your car stopped by the side of the freeway and didn't move. I got my boys together and came out to see what happened." She gives an unladylike snort. My fists clench. "Instead of accusing me, I think you should say a fuckin' thank you."

"Thank you for kidnapping me?" She tosses back her hair, but the gesture's not so impressive when she needs to put a hand to her head.

Despite my legendary control, my temper starts to rise. "I didn't fuckin' kidnap you. I rescued you from those who tried to and brought you back here where you'd be safe."

"So…" She advances on me again. This time, though, it's to poke a finger in my chest. "If I'm not your prisoner, why the locked door? If you give me a phone, I'll call my dad."

I grab her hand. My jaw is tight as I refuse. "That I can't do."

"I don't understand why you're keeping me here." That she's completely at my mercy seems to dawn on her as any lingering hope as well as her bravado falls away from her face. She turns her back toward me. Her shoulders shake, and her head bows. "Rolo was in the car."

It's a statement, not a plea for sympathy.

"I know," I tell her, softly.

Her back straightens, but her voice sounds choked. "You left my dog to die."

Her car burst into flames before we left. If Rolo had still been there, there would have been nothing that we could do.

My voice hardens. "You really think I'm that much of a bastard, don't you? You think I'd run your car off the road, risk hurting you, then leave your fuckin' dog to die? You think that little of me?"

Her shoulders rise and fall. "I don't think. I know."

"Look at me." When she doesn't comply, I state my request once again. "I said, look at me." She's stubborn as a fucking mule, I decide, as she refuses to comply. I take a step closer, put my hand on her shoulder, and swing her around.

"Stop manhandling me," she protests, then notices I've unzipped my jacket, and sees the little head poking out. Her eyes go large. "*Rolo?*"

I let the now squirming bundle free of the confines of my coat, where she'd made herself comfortable. She goes to her mistress. Then I watch, detached, as Ruby drops to the floor, clutching the tiny dog to her.

"Remember, Princess, you don't know me at all. You have no fuckin' idea what I'm capable of, or the lengths that I will go to. But I assure you, I have not kidnapped you. You hear me?"

She nuzzles Rolo's fur, seeming to find it hard to accept she's really holding her. "For this, for bringing me her, I will thank you. But if you didn't kidnap me, then why didn't you take me to a hospital, or at least take me home? And why is the door locked? Why aren't I free to go?"

Breathing deeply, I bow my head and rub at my temples. Her attitude makes me angry, but it's the position her father's put both me and her in that incenses me. Why should I stand here taking all the blame?

Making a rapid decision, I take my phone from my pocket and press on his number.

"Brewster. It's Toad. Your daughter wants to speak to you." Ignoring his blustering, I pass the phone across.

Ruby grabs it like a lifeline. "Daddy, I..." Her lips purse. "You know?... Yes, I think I'm fine. I banged my head, got bruised up... What do you mean Toad called you?" Her eyes narrow as they turn my way. "I'm on the Wicked Warriors compound. Can you get Masters to fetch me and bring me home?... What?" Now her jaw drops. "What do you mean I'm safest here for now?" Her face flushes red. "Do everything Toad tells me to do? You've got to be kidding me." Her features contort with rage. "No. I'm not staying here. I'll find my own way back." She stabs at the red key and ends the call.

Her chest heaves as she takes a breath. "You can't make me stay here."

Oh, Ruby, I'm going to do a lot worse. But that, for now, I keep to myself.

"Didn't you listen to your dad?" I might have only heard her side of the call, but I could fill in the gaps. "You need to stay here, Princess."

"Rolo and I are leaving."

"No, Princess." My voice is as firm as hers.

"Give me one reason why I should listen to you!"

She's riled, annoyed at being thwarted, upset at being told what to do. Her eyes blaze, her cheeks flare, stubborn lines appear on her forehead. Her chest heaves, drawing my attention to those breasts which I'd love to lavish attention on, if they came in a willing package of course.

Words would be my defence, my explanation. But how can I tell her the truth of what her father had done? The knowledge would destroy her. To hear she was sold at birth, and that today she narrowly escaped being taken and kept by an evil drug lord; there's no kind way to explain that to her.

As her hands clench at her sides, her eyes open in challenge, her mouth twists in preparation to slay me with remonstrations again, I lose my goddamn senses. I approach fast, my hand shooting out and wrapping into her hair. Careful to avoid her recent injury, I tug her toward me and crash my mouth down on hers.

Her hands try to push me away, but with my free hand, I clamp her to me. She bites my lip. I taste blood, but take advantage, sweeping my tongue in to meet hers. A growl comes from her throat, but I'm relentless. I push her back until she hits the wall.

A wealth of frustration burns through me. I'm as trapped as much as her by the promises made by her father. She doesn't want me. Intellectually, I don't want her. But physically? She's spirited, fearless, wild and untamed and that does something to me. All at once, I want to be the one who tames her, who brings her to her knees and has her begging for me to give her my cock.

She gives up pushing at me. Instead, her hands rise, her nails digging into my cheeks. I continue to move my mouth against hers, my tongue plundering. She keeps fighting.

Heaven forgive me, but she's turning me on. I push my pelvis against her, letting her feel my erection.

Releasing my hold of her hair, I sweep up both my hands and grab hers, anchoring them to the wall behind us.

My body trapping her, but gently, wary of her cracked ribs, I draw back my head. "You can't fight me," I tell her.

I feel the moment her rage turns to fear and I back up immediately. She stays in position, leaning back against the wall, but now her flushed cheeks are not of arousal and any desire on my part switches off immediately.

I stare at her before insisting, "When you come to my bed, you'll come willingly."

"What?" Now free, her fear retreats and her spirit rises again. Her eyes flare. A step forward brings her close enough to slap my face hard. "Never," she spits at me, her chest heaving.

But her pupils are dilated and underneath her indignation, I believe I also read interest. Rubbing my cheek—she didn't hold back—I consider we might not like each other, but there's an undeniable physical attraction from my part at least, and maybe from hers. Maybe marriage wouldn't resemble a prison sentence.

"Princess." I approach her again, but my hands are splayed as if calming a wild animal. I gentle my voice, placing my knuckles under her chin, raising her face. "We've both got shit coming that neither of us will like, but we'll have to make the most of it."

"I don't understand." She jerks her head away from my touch.

I'm tired of this. Tired of fighting with her. I pull away, running my hands through my hair, pushing it back from my face. Why the fuck did I agree to protect her father when it's him that's causing her pain? I'm just another innocent party. I should be able to tell her the truth.

I pace to one side of the small room and then back, stopping just in front of her. I lower my gaze to look her straight in the eye. "Those men today, the ones who ran you off the road? They were coming for you, and they'll keep coming."

She glances to the side and takes a deep breath. "Because they want to kidnap me and expect my dad to pay a ransom?"

If only it was that easy. "Close, but no cigar," I tell her, grinding my teeth.

Whichever way I look at it, Ruby's not a woman who's easily led. If she doesn't know the truth, she'd never give in. I lower my eyes and look her straight in the face. "You might be kidnapped but no ransom will be asked for. You see, you yourself are the prize."

"What the hell are you talking about?"

I look at her, really look at her, seeing the physical pain in her eyes that bravely she's been trying to hide. Bruised ribs are hell to deal with, and then there's that bump on her head. Feeling compassion, I gesture to the bed. "Sit down, and I'll tell you all of it."

CHAPTER 6

RUBY

What's going on?

I stare at Toad, unsure whether I want to sit in close proximity and talk. There's no doubt he's withholding information from me. Information, I suspect, I need to know. But since he'd walked into this room, sucking all the air out of it, I've been off kilter. *Why does this man affect me so?*

He's hardly done anything to gain my confidence. One minute, we were screaming at each other, the next? *He'd kissed me.*

And heaven forgive me, for a moment, I liked it.

I may not be the princess that he keeps calling me, but I'm a woman who deserves respect. All my boyfriends have been sweethearts, asking permission, if not verbally, but with tentative approaches before they'd dared put their lips to mine. No one's ever demanded or taken from me. Until him.

I'd fought Toad, then weakened, maybe even unbelievably starting to enjoy it, before I grew scared he'd want more than I was prepared to give. Toad's no boy, and he hadn't asked for consent. But once it was obvious I wasn't giving it, he'd stepped back. When he made that preposterous suggestion that I'd willingly go to his bed, I'd slapped him for his audacity, then immediately regretted it. But despite my fear, he didn't attempt to hit back.

My violence, something I'm not known for, if I'm honest, was driven by the feelings he'd roused in me. Not just from that kiss, but the thought he invoked of he and I on a horizontal surface. It scared me how there was a big part of me that wanted that. For the first time ever, I'd felt something I'd only read about. *Arousal.* For a brief moment, it made me understand why women are tempted to take a walk on the wild side.

I must have hit my head very, very hard. A man like him and a woman like me shouldn't be in a room together, let alone a bed. Leaving aside my dislike for him, Toad's not in my class. He's so far beneath me it's unbelievable.

I came here scared, believing I had been kidnapped. Now I know, Toad's my rescuer, but things still don't make sense. He's told me the men after me are likely to try again, and I've no idea what they're after, if it's not money they want.

My head is still throbbing from where I hit it, and I think the painkillers are wearing off. That I obey his suggestion to sit on the bed is more to do with my various aches than through any thought of obeying him. I want to know what he's talking about, why he is so positive the men after me will try again. Just what is going on between him and my father?

Even when I comply, Toad doesn't seem eager to begin an explanation. He walks to the barred window and looks out, then taps his hands on the frame. He leans his head forward, so it touches the bars.

"You need more painkillers?" He glances back at me.

I do, but I need something more. "I need you to start talking."

He turns back to resume staring at the view outside, which, as I've found out, only looks onto the back of their garage. Nothing to warrant his studious attention.

Digging my fingernails into my palms, I force myself to stay quiet. I already know Toad is a match for me verbally, and it's as easy for me to get him riled as it is for him to annoy me. If I want to learn what's going on, it will be on his own time. I have to be patient.

From outside, a few voices sound. From this distance, I'm

unable to hear the precise words spoken. Then there's a hearty laugh.

That seems to spur Toad on, as he suddenly turns, his eyes drawn, and his demeanour suggests he's tired.

"You've got choices, Princess. One, you accept all that I'm asking, and don't question the reason. Or two, you ask me to break a promise." His eyes half shutter as if that pains him. "Breaking my promise means taking the risk that your relationship with your dad will be destroyed irrevocably."

It's on the tip of my tongue to tell him of course I want to know when his seriousness gets to me.

I like being who I am. Who wouldn't? I get everything I want handed to me. I'm spoilt, even I acknowledge it. But my dad likes spoiling me, and I enjoy being the recipient. With no mom, I depend on the man who was responsible for my birth, and with only me, he's equally dependent on me.

I love my life, even though I've not yet decided what to make of it and enjoy the existence I have with my dad.

What if Toad's right? What if the next words out of his mouth will destroy all of it?

Rolo snuggles up in my lap, licking my hand as I automatically stroke her. *Is there anything Toad could stay that would make me stop loving my dad?* Nothing, I'm sure of it. With new confidence, I make my decision.

"Tell me everything, Toad. All of it."

He looks down at his hands, then raises his eyes. He seems to be examining me carefully. Then he sighs, and like a man defeated, comes to the bed and sits beside me, but keeps a respectful distance between us.

"The relationship between this MC and your dad goes back years," he starts, surprising me from the outset.

For the next half hour, I go through the entire spectrum of possible emotions. When the tears start and Toad inches closer, putting his arm around me, I lean into him. When the implications hit of how much my dad must have hated me from the start, I clutch at his cut, and cry against him.

When finally, the hateful words stop, and Toad says no more, my mind starts racing.

Sitting up, I brush away my tears. Toad hands me a tissue, and I blow my nose and dab at my eyes.

"Daddy loves me," I tell him without hesitation.

"He does." Toad's agreement comes fast.

"He must have been distraught when he made that arrangement."

Again, Toad nods. "And out of his mind. He didn't know you then, but you've grown into your own person."

My father had been stupid, no more than that. But now his mistakes are coming back to bite him, and it's looks like it's me who's going to have to pay the price.

My choices Toad had put simply. Either fulfil my father's end of the bargain, or marry the prez of the Wicked Warriors MC.

"I'll leave," I tell Toad with determination. I certainly don't want to be taken by the cartel, nor do I want my father to stand up against them. As for tying myself to Toad? The thought's completely preposterous. "Then Daddy won't be blamed, and I'll be out of their reach."

Toad's eyes go wide. "You know how big a reach the cartel has?"

"I could go to England. Italy, France. Anywhere in the world."

He doesn't dismiss it immediately. To give him his due, he seems to be considering it. I suppose it's an out for him as well as me. He might believe I think I'm a prize as I come with money, but that's all I really have. My arrogance hides the persona of a shy, insecure girl inside. When my father had dissuaded me from going to college, it wasn't laziness that kept me by his side, but concern about how I'd fare out in the world.

Toad might not know it yet, but if this ludicrous suggestion of a relationship between us comes to fruition, he'd be getting the worst end of the deal. Though nothing would drag that truth out of me.

"What I can't understand, is why Enrico wants me? I'm nothing special."

Toad sits back, his eyes assessing me. "I'd have to contradict you on that score." His words make my cheeks heat, but I've no time to process any deeper meaning. "But however you turned out, don't forget, Enrico signed this contract when you were a baby." He pauses, and his eyes glaze. I gather he's thinking. "Enrico's had your dad in his pocket for twenty-one years."

I stare at him as I process his words. "If what you're saying is true, then Daddy probably knows everything about Enrico's business. Daddy's made no secret that he wants to retire. In that case, Enrico could be scared that he'd lose control over him. Control he retains if Enrico has me."

I'm trying to get my head around the fact that Daddy is a criminal, as much, if not more, than the man who's currently comforting me. Toad was right. I don't know who my father is anymore. Sure, he might have changed his mind, discovered love for a daughter he hadn't wanted, but that doesn't change how he's lied all my life. I'd never had choices. My future was preordained at the point of my birth.

The house where I live, the clothes that I wear, everything down to the food put on our table has been bought with dirty money. At least Toad honestly wears the badge of his criminality with the cut on his back.

Toad's looking at me astutely. "I wouldn't be surprised if Enrico set this up as an insurance package when you were born. Once your dad signed on the dotted line, he was always tied to Enrico. One thing I'm certain of is there's no escape. He won't stop looking for you, wherever you go."

I swallow, then broach the hardest part of what Toad has

just told me. "Then nothing will stop him. Why you, Toad? Why should…" I can hardly bring myself to put together the words that sound so wrong to me. "Why should marriage to you make any difference?"

He sighs and places his head in his hands. He draws his fingers down his face, elongating his eyes before looking at me. "Firstly, because I'm the man crazy enough to agree to take you on. You," he gives a quick grin, "have a reputation."

"With the money Dad's willing to pay, I think I could marry just about anyone," I retort. Sure, I'm difficult. I cultivate it. Holding my nose in the air means I have to meet no one's eye. I don't need to make polite conversation as it isn't expected. I can easily hide that I'm just a scared child inside.

Rolo rolls over, stretches, and traitor that she is, leaves my lap for his. Idly, Toad strokes her. "Enrico prefers you a virgin and pure. Your daddy's words, not mine," he adds quickly, as if he's not right to assume one way or another about just how well my father knows me. "But at the end of the day, it's you he wants, and he'll have you anyway he can take you."

"So even marrying you wouldn't be a way out. He'd just come for me anyway. He wouldn't care who stands in his way."

"Not when it's my club," Toad says with certainty. "And not me. He wouldn't want to go up against me."

"Why not?" I tilt my head, regarding him curiously.

He chuckles. "Because we know where the bodies are buried. The Wicked Warriors have chapters all over the country. He declares war on me, and he'll be out of his depth."

"Because you're a bigger criminal?"

He growls. "I don't traffic women, nor distribute drugs likely to kill people. Don't talk about me in the same breath as that man."

"What does your club do?" While there's no way on earth I could agree to this proposal, I'm curious about the man who seems to be offering his hand in marriage as a favour, not as a declaration of undying love. Apart from the benevolence of my father, I can't see what he gets out of it at all. To me, five million dollars doesn't seem enough.

"What do we do?" He chuckles. "Club business, doll, and nothing to do with you. But I can tell you, we run a gentlemen's club, a tattoo parlour, and have a lot where we buy and sell cars and bikes."

"All brought to you hotwired, I suspect," I snap, unable to help myself.

"There she is." Toad smirks at me. "Your judgemental self disappeared for a while."

Well, I'm back now. I turn my back on him but continue to speak, "I can't marry you or Enrico. It's the twenty-first century. Women aren't bought and sold. I'll go to the cops, tell them everything."

"And you think they'll believe you? What's going on in your head, sweetheart? You think everyone will bow down to you? Your father's hated by the cops because he runs rings around them. They're hardly likely to help you."

I stomp my foot. Literally. I know I'm behaving like a child, but honestly, all this is the stupidest stuff I've ever heard. "I can't marry you. I don't even like you."

As I turn away, out of the side of my eye, I see him shrug. "Can't say I care much for you either." He grins. "Sounds like the perfect match. Neither of us have expectations and we both know where we stand."

"Why are you called Toad?" I suddenly ask, then scoff, waving my hand at his body. "Is it because you're so damn ugly? Are you covered in warts?"

"Warts an' all." He laughs, taking no umbrage. His hands move to the bottom of his t-shirt and grip it. "Want me to bare the goods and show you?"

"No," I squeal, sounding like a woman from a couple of centuries back faced with the prospect of a naked man on her wedding night. I realise my comparison is too close for comfort, and there's a little part of me that really would like to see what he looks like under his clothes. I have no idea why. Is this what Stockholm syndrome feels like? Being swept in by a kidnapper's charms?

I snort, covering it up as a cough. Toad's got no charms. And there's certainly nothing of his that I want to see.

At that moment, his phone rings. He holds up his hand, points to the door, then takes himself outside.

Tiptoeing after him, I try to listen to his conversation. He's speaking quietly, so I can't make much out. Toad murmurs on for a few moments, then I pick up a couple of *uh-huhs* and a barked snort of, *he expects you to pay the price you agreed, what did you expect?*

Then he says, "Yeah, I'll let you talk to her." I hear his boots clomp on the floor, and I hastily move back across the room.

As if he has x-ray vision, he does that annoying smirk again when he comes back in. He holds out his phone to me. "Daddy wants to talk to you."

My hand trembles as I take it. "Daddy?" My voice isn't steady at all.

"Ruby, baby, I know Toad's told you everything, and I know you must hate me now. But I can't risk Enrico taking you. I need you safe. You've got to marry Toad. Today."

"Today?" I squeak.

"It needn't be forever, Ruby. Just to give me time to get Enrico off my back. He's in the country and he's coming for you. The only way I can keep both of us safe is to say you married without me knowing. Faced with a fait accompli, he might back off."

This is preposterous. "Perhaps I should meet Enrico and make my choice. He can't be any worse than Toad." I narrow my eyes at the man I've named and wait for his reaction.

He doesn't seem bothered in the least, as if it's no skin off his nose if I choose someone else.

I think it's that that makes me realise he's doing me a favour, rather than my dad who can have no excuses for bringing me to this crossroads in my life. I realise now, he's not the person I need to talk to. Daddy got me into this mess, it seems only Toad can get me out. And if we are going through with this sham of a marriage, there have to be rules put in place.

"I'll speak to you later, Dad. I need to talk to Toad."

CHAPTER 7

TOAD

It hasn't been lost on me that she's been in a car accident today. Her head and ribs must be causing her pain, but she's not complained once. There's only been a few winces. which she tried to cover up. Despite myself, I've been impressed with how she's handling it all so coolly.

Maybe she's got no emotion at all, is just as shallow as she appears, or maybe, she's got hidden depths. I didn't agree to this charade with anything other than hopes she'd be good enough to keep my dick satisfied in bed. Out of it, our lives wouldn't cross much. She could go on doing whatever the fuck socialites do, and I'd get on with my role as MC prez. But now I'm starting to wonder what she'd be like if I take the time to really know her.

She's got a backbone I didn't expect.

She should be scared, terrified, but she's not.

When she hands me back my phone, she's biting her lip, but not out of nervousness. It appears more as an aid to her thinking. Her brow furrows and her eyes narrow. Not wanting to interrupt her train of thought, I inch back until the door's behind me and I fold my arms.

When she speaks, I listen.

"How much time have we got?"

I wince, wishing that's not what she'd started with. "None at all," I reply, honestly. "That's what your dad was telling me. Having failed with your kidnapping today, Enrico's put the pressure on your father. He's arriving tomorrow and is demanding your presence. And your trousseau."

"My trousseau?" She snorts with startled laughter. "That's a word I didn't expect to come out of the mouth of a biker."

Letting my shoulders rise and fall, I shake my head. "Whatever you want to take to start your married life in Mexico, if you want me to give it to you straight."

A strange look crosses her face. "Then it's already too late. There's no way we can get married between now and tomorrow."

"I've got the licence already. I got it when this crazy idea was first planned, and your dad bribed the judge to stay as late as it takes. Don't worry, Ruby, we can be wed by tonight."

She frowns, and I wait for her next objection. "I have a reputation… No, don't laugh. I don't mean the one where I'm difficult." She gives a half-smile. "I mean, I've a social following. To make people believe it, my wedding should be all over Facebook and Instagram."

Yeah, I know that. Cloud, our computer guy, named for having his head in virtual cloud storage, has already warned me of that. But I see that as extra protection for her. After her "happy" marriage, Enrico won't be able to appear with her on his arm.

"I understand. There'll be pictures we can post."

Her brows rise. "Showing me wearing a dress covered in blood?"

I've already thought of that. "You got a personal shopper?" I try not to regard her disdainfully, but from her blush, I don't succeed. "You've got someone who knows your measurements and can shop for your clothes?"

Her flushed cheeks make me wonder if they'll be that colour when she comes. But again, to give her her due, she doesn't deny she's too lazy to choose her own attire. Instead, she gets on my wavelength.

"I do. And I can have a wedding dress here in an hour."

For the first time today, I feel some of the weight lifted from me. She seems to have stopped fighting and has gotten on board. Whether it's become a game, something to occupy her mind while she plots to escape me, I can't quite decide. But she'll have no chance to run. She might not have her friends at the wedding, but I'll have mine. My whole fucking club will be with me.

"Can I borrow your phone?" She holds out her hand.

Passing it over, I hover close by, ready to snatch it off her if she places a call for help. But she doesn't. She first rings Masters and asks him to look up a number for her, then when it comes to my phone via text, she calls that next.

It's to someone called Delia, and I watch as Ruby's face transforms as she speaks to her.

I hadn't been aware up until that moment, that a mask had fallen from her face over the past couple of hours, but when she speaks to her personal shopper, it comes back up. A superficial aura starts to surround her as she speaks in nasal tones, demanding, not requesting, that Delia drop everything else.

A dress, stockings, underwear and shoes are all ordered. A veil? She glances at me, and I think, why the fuck not? There's something appealing about lifting lace, revealing my eager bride to me that the Neanderthal inside me seems to like, so I grin and nod.

Then frown. What the fuck does she need my size for?

I give her the basic details of what I buy when I grab a few new t-shirts and my waist size. Leg length? Long enough to straddle my bike comfortably, but that doesn't seem to be what she wants.

When she orders a fucking tux, I hold up my hands.

"Whoa. No one's getting me in a monkey suit. I'll wear jeans and my cut."

She holds the phone away from her mouth and cocks her head. "No shirt?"

Bare chested at my wedding? "You like that thought?" I

leer at her. It seems I've lost some of my effect on her, as instead of her horrified exclamation, she giggles.

"Much as I might like to see that, I'm my father's daughter."

She's right, but she's marrying a biker. "Pants," I relent. "And a white button-up shirt, but no tie, and none of that fancy stuff."

And I'll still be wearing my cut. And my motorcycle boots.

After asking me for the address, she ends the call, giving the clearly startled shopper details of where to deliver the stuff she's ordered.

"Done," she announces, looking pleased with herself. Then, to my surprise, her pleasure at spending money she's not earned is not sustained and quickly comes to an end.

"Is this real?" she asks, almost in a whisper. "Am I really getting married today?"

I grimace. I might not like her, but a girl only gets one first wedding day. It should be special for her. She should have her handsome prince, not a man like me. It won't matter how often she kisses me, this Toad will never be able to hand over the keys to a kingdom. I doubt very much that a motorcycle club counts.

"My face, Toad." There's a tear in her eye as she gingerly touches her cheek. "I must look awful."

The answer comes to me in a second, and I know it's going to be one she hates.

"I know just the people who can help."

My original intention had been to keep her locked in this room until it was time for our nuptials, but my frame of mind has altered from when I first entered. Then, I was facing an imperious woman who wouldn't even deign to thank me for favours I'd performed.

Having to marry me, a man so far beneath her, was a punishment from one of my kind to one of hers—a slap in the face, a finger raised at the way she'd been brought up, and her expectations of everything being given to her on a plate. I wanted to punish her because I was facing paying a penance myself.

I never wanted an old lady. I was perfectly happy with the club whores and the hangarounds who couldn't get enough of a biker. As for kids? While it would help her case, it wasn't something I'd ever seen on my horizon.

It has taken me by surprise to catch glimpses of a woman who appeals to me, someone I might be tempted to have a relationship with, even if I weren't being forced. The memory of that kiss, well, yes, I'd forced that intimacy onto her, but I hadn't been able to stop myself. Something strange had come over me, overruling my normally iron control. When our lips met, my cock had swelled, and I'd sensed she wasn't completely immune to me.

Things which previously had seemed impossible, now rise to the surface as having possibilities heretofore never thought of. There's a risk in showing her who I am, and what life with me would look like.

Would it be worse for her to be thrown into the deep end *after* my ring is on her finger?

I wonder what she's really made of, and whether that mask she wears is her true self.

As she looks at me, her head tilted as though expecting me to produce a seasoned makeup artist out of thin air, I come to a decision. She can't run, she has no option. And there might just be a chance that underneath it all, she's a woman who despite the odds, might fit into my life.

"Come with me."

"Like this?" She waves down at her body, drawing my attention to how she looks. I've kind of gotten used to her bloodied appearance, but now it dawns on me it's not the way she'd like to present herself.

When treating her injuries, Scalpel had obviously sponged off her face, but her dress? It's ruined.

"Your man gave me this to wear." She spins on her heels and picks up, with not a little distaste, some balled-up clothing from the floor. I suppress my mirth as she shakes it out and shows me what Scalpel had given to her. It's a Wicked Warrior's t-shirt.

When she holds it against her slender body with a sharp twist to her mouth, I nod at her. "That'll do."

Her eyes open comically. "But he gave me no pants."

"Princess, it's long enough to cover all the necessities." Making the obvious comparison, I add, "Not much shorter than that dress you're wearing." As she narrows her eyes, her expression suggesting if she had a gun in her hand she'd kill me, I shrug. "It's up to you. My brothers aren't going to give a damn what you're wearing."

The bizarre thought enters my head that if they spend too much time looking at her shapely legs, I'll kill them. Stunned by my sudden burst of possessiveness, I shake that thought off. To her, my outward expression remains impassive.

For a moment, there's a staring match between us, but, as expected, eventually I win.

"Turn around," she instructs, holding the shirt as though it's armour in front of her.

I do, while thinking it's our wedding day, and hopefully later, I'll get a chance to see all the deliciousness she's hiding from me. So for now, while I'm no gentleman, I'm gentlemanly enough, not to sneak a peek at her. Though my cock jerks at the thought of her semi-naked behind me.

She'll be mine.

Why the fuck does that send shivers through me?

"I'm ready." There's a slight shake to her voice as if stripping herself of her dress, which probably cost thousands, has removed some shield. If I'm honest though, as I turn to see her wearing my club's shirt, the sight does something to me. It screams out that she belongs to me. And that, apparently, is something that appeals to my inner caveman.

I hold out my elbow, again in a gentlemanly fashion, wondering what kind of spell she's put on me.

She puts her hand gently on my arm. I start to walk, but she holds me back. Quirking a brow at her, I ask a nonverbal question.

Her mouth twists as though she hates betraying a weakness. "Can I get some painkillers? The last have worn off."

Scalpel will definitely have some shit to keep her going, but I'll have to vet what he gives her as I don't want her unconscious.

Patting her hand, I tell her, "Let's get you sorted."

I take a deep breath and lead her out of the back room where it's quiet, along the corridor and then we emerge into the heart of my clubhouse.

When she comes to a halt beside me, I inwardly wince, seeing it through her eyes. It's dingy, with dark nicotine-stained walls and ceiling, a mismatch of tables and chairs, an elderly jukebox, an ancient pool table, and a long bar. Rock music is playing, thankfully not too loudly, but even so, I very much doubt it's to her taste.

Seeing Scalpel standing by the bar, I head straight for him. He hears my footsteps and spins around when I draw close.

His medic's eyes examine her carefully, and thankfully he doesn't appear to notice her legs. When he reaches out a hand to brush back her hair, obviously to check that her stitches show no sign of infection, I can't help myself. I slap his hand away.

He barks a laugh. "Like that, is it, Prez?"

Clamping my lips closed to stop my mouth dropping open at my own actions, I question myself as to what has made me suddenly so possessive. Then I dismiss it. I'm a dog with a bone, that's all. Someone gives it to me, tells me it's mine, and I'll hang on to the darn thing even if I don't like it.

Astutely he asks, "You need more painkillers?"

Princess grimaces. "Please."

He takes a bottle out of his pocket and taps a couple of tablets into his hand. When I raise my eyebrow, he explains, "Tramadol."

At least that shit's got a name. Some of the other stuff he supplies is more dubious, but it does the trick. I've seen some brothers high as a fucking kite while he digs for a bullet or sets a broken bone.

I rap the bar smartly, getting the attention of Punchbag, our latest prospect. We normally give out road names when a man patches in, but he'd earned his early. We'd thrown him in the ring to see what he was made of, and as it turns out, it wasn't anything. If it hadn't been for him standing his ground and not wimping out, no matter how many times he was hit, he wouldn't still be wearing the prospect patch. He might have worked on improving his skills, but the name will stick with him.

"Water," I snap when I get his attention.

"I'd rather have a strong drink," Princess comments.

"Not on those painkillers," I warn her, while Scalpel just shrugs. Shortly, she needs to stand up beside me and say her vows. I can't afford for her to be comatose. I turn back to the prospect. "Go drag the girls out of bed, will you?"

As I issue the instruction, and he smartly leaps to attention and runs off to action it, I question whether I know what I'm doing.

Princess is about to get initiated into some of the less savoury aspects of the club.

CHAPTER 8

RUBY

I've been brought up in luxury all my life. When I've gone out, it's been to swanky hotels or restaurants, or nightclubs where normal folks have to stand in line to get in, while my ID gets me to the front of the line and straight into the VIP area.

I have never been in a place like the Wicked Warriors MC's clubhouse before.

It's the aroma that hits me first—lingering cigarette smoke, stale beer, and underneath that, the odour of something earthy. At my first lungful, I baulked, but while I wouldn't say it's appealing, there's something honest about it.

Feeling out of my depth, I cling on to Toad's arm as he leads me deeper into his domain, and keep my eyes focused on the man I do recognise, their medic.

It's only when he names what he's giving me that I realise how vulnerable I am. These men could give anything to me, *do* anything to me. Even recognising the brand, I'm still nervous when the tablets are placed in my hand, and Toad asks an eager, younger man, for some water.

What the hell am I doing?

But despite how he'd kissed me earlier, I don't get the feeling that Toad would rape me. And if he was going to, he's man enough to overpower me without any help from date-rape drugs. So I swallow the tablets back and hope for the best. The best being I'll be able to breathe easier and this thumping pain in my head will go away.

I'm getting married in less than two hours.

It suddenly dawns on me that having Toad's ring on my

finger won't be the worst thing to happen to me today. I'll be his, no longer my daddy's girl, and I won't be going home.

Suddenly I turn to him. "Where do you live, Toad?"

He looks confused for a second, then gestures around him. "Here."

Oh God, no. I start to back away from him, shaking my head from side to side. "I can't, Toad. I just, can't." Who will do my hair? Who will prepare my food for me? Who will make sure my car's brought around to the front of the house whenever I need it?

As if he's a mind reader, Toad starts to advance. For each step I take back, he takes one forward. Eventually, my back comes up against something solid.

Wishing I could disappear through the wall like a ghost, I look around him, trying to spy an escape route. But while the room isn't crowded, it is occupied by a few men, all of whom, I suspect, will stop me. I hold on to Rolo as if she's a lifeline, feeling relieved as she snuggles into my chest.

Toad, more gently than I think he's capable of, cups a hand to my cheek. It's calloused, and before him, I'd never felt anything like it. Daddy and most men I know pride themselves on their manicures.

"You can, Princess," he tells me, his voice low but compelling. "You can do anything that you want. You've never had a chance to find yourself, so why not grab it now?" He strokes my face, so softly, I find myself leaning into his caress. "This may be a lot rougher than you're used to, but you'll find us amenable enough if you give us a chance."

"I can't cook," I admit, though why I chose that to announce I'm not certain.

He chuckles. "Then you're lucky. Dwarf doesn't often allow anyone into his kitchen. It might not come on fancy plates or with solid silver cutlery, but don't worry, Princess. You'll be fed."

"I like vegetables." God, I sound so childish, but I remember too well how at dinner he'd eschewed them.

He snorts a laugh. "We're not allergic to them." He flexes his impressive muscles, drawing my attention to his bulging arms and his mass of tattoos. "We don't put crap fuel in our bikes, so why should we put it in our bodies?" He chuckles softly. "Midnight isn't much for eating greens, but I swear Dwarf disguises them for him."

But who's going to count my calories?

Who's going to make sure my diet is nutritious?

"Princess," he continues in that voice that seems mesmerizing. "You can do, be whoever you want."

Be whoever I want? Up to now, I've just been Daddy's daughter.

To become someone in my own right? The thought is both scary and exhilarating at the same time. Though, it comes with a big but.

"You'll expect me to behave like your wife." Or that's my experience of men, anyway, taken from the many business associates of my father who'd graced our table along with their wives. Expectations of behaviour rewarded with a comfortable life; affection withheld for anything other.

He moves his fingers and taps my nose. "You know, Princess? I'm kind of considering you right now as a chrysalis. Who knows what kind of butterfly you'll be when you emerge? And," he taps me again, "I've even got a feeling I might like the result."

"You don't like me," I remind him, also telling myself, I hate him and his sort. Though it's getting harder for me to remember it.

The revelations about my father, even worse than how he'd bartered me away at birth, mean that he's never been honest with me. My whole existence has been based on a lie. Daddy isn't an upstanding citizen. He's a criminal. The difference between him and Toad, is that Toad is honest about it.

"Hey," Toad says. "Come meet some of my men." His sharp eyes bore into me. "If you withhold your judgement, you might even get on with them."

Quickly throwing a glance behind him, I see several men, some sneaking looks in our direction as though curious about the interloper brought into their midst. On first inspection, I decide they could never be my friends. Like Toad, they're wearing leather vests, t-shirts and jeans which seem covered in dirt. Many are bearded, while I prefer men to be clean-shaven.

It's one of the things I don't like about Toad.

Though his appearance is slowly growing on me.

I called him ugly, but maybe that's wrong. His face is weathered and bears scars, but maybe, just maybe, there's some attractiveness as to how his features are arranged.

I'm falling under his spell.

As I wonder what magic he's weaving, I let him take me by the hand and lead me across the room to where three men are seated.

One of them kicks out a chair, but Toad prevents me taking it, pulling my back to his front, and wrapping his arms firmly around me. I notice at once I feel safe, as if the metaphor he'd just used really fits me, like a chrysalis in its cocoon.

"Raider," Toad states. "My VP." One of the men raises his chin at me.

He's watching me in such a calculating way, I immediately feel unbalanced. Men normally jump to their feet after they're introduced to me, knowing immediately who, and what, I am. I sense Raider knows as little about me, as I do about him. When I attempt a small smile, his face relaxes.

"Metalhead," Toad speaks again. This time, the man so addressed, gives me a little salute. "He's my sergeant-at-arms, and he keeps us all safe."

"I try to." Metalhead's voice is even gruffer than Toad's.

"And you'll be making my job easier if you always do what I say." When he sees me stiffen, he shakes his head as if I've taken it the wrong way. "You're one of us now, Princess. It's my job to keep you out of harm's way."

"With that fucker Enrico on the loose, you'd do best to agree," the third man barks, then softens his face. "I'm Cloud. I'm your go-to tech guy."

"And who's that?" Raider points to the little head poking out from my crossed arms.

"Rolo," I answer, emphasising, "my dog." I wait for him to call her a rat or give one of the many insults I've heard her referred to.

"Cute little thing. Hey, put her down." Toad makes the decision for me, prying my arms open and placing Rolo gently on the floor. Raider snaps his fingers and little traitor that she is, she runs straight to him.

"Bet a mutt like that cost a fuckin' fortune," Metalhead remarks.

"Yeah, fools and their money are easily parted." Raider rolls his eyes, while with just one finger, he strokes her under her chin.

This is one topic I can speak on for hours. I'm spirited when I respond, "I agree. Some fool bought her for his little girl who treated her like a toy. When I rescued her, it took me months to get her to trust anyone again. She's going to have health problems ahead of her because of how she's been bred. It's a crime what they do to get designer dogs." My breathing's sped up by the time I've finished with my tirade.

Toad stiffens, turns me in his arms, and says, "Come again, Princess?"

I'm getting onto my bandwagon. "Chihuahuas are small, but not *that* small. She's been purposefully bred that way. It's wrong—"

When Toad's lips slam down onto mine, my breath is taken away. I should protest, should push him off me, but do

I do that? No, I respond, letting his tongue slide into my mouth. When he quickly pulls back, I try to clutch him to me, before remembering myself and letting my arms drop.

Embarrassed, I turn away from him, only to be faced by three faces instead. I look down at the floor to avoid seeing censure, or amusement in their eyes.

"She'll do, Toad," Metalhead states.

"Yeah. Does she know the work we do breaking up dog fighting rings?"

I turn fast, looking at Toad. "You break them up?"

Toad grins. "Yeah, I've got a friend, Snoops, who thinks much as you do. We bust rings, rescue the dogs, and Snoops cares for them and rehomes them."

Words come into my head and out of my mouth before I can stop them. "I think I could love you just for that." I redden and quickly look away from him.

He seems just as flummoxed as I am, as he gives a chin lift to the three seated men, takes my hand and pulls me away.

"Come meet the others." Purposefully, he seems to ignore what I've just said.

At the pool table, there are two men standing, holding cues, with the balls scattered over the table.

One's got dark sleek hair tied back in a long braid that reaches almost down to his ass. He leans over the table and takes a shot. When his ball bounces away from the pocket, he shakes his head, steps back, then approaches.

"Midnight," he introduces himself.

"Navajo?" I ask.

He gives a nod.

"I'm Bonk, if anyone's interested." Bonk, unlike Midnight, has successfully potted his shot. He moves on to line up his next.

As if me successfully identifying his heritage has bonded us, Midnight, confides, "Bonkers by name, Bonkers by nature."

Bonk doesn't seem at all offended. "Nice to meet you, Princess," he throws at me, before concentrating on potting the next ball.

So far, all I've seen in the clubhouse have been men. When I hear female voices, I turn.

"Prez." One stifles a yawn though it's only mid-afternoon. "You wanted us?"

She's dressed in a skimpy dress which barely reaches her thighs and is obviously braless. As I watch, she makes a show of trying to put a rebellious boob back inside the bodice.

The second one is dressed much the same, and she reaches out her hand and places it on Toad's arm in a proprietary way which immediately has me stiffening.

"You up for some fun, Prez?" Not content with her simple touch, she sidles up to him, brushing against him like a cat.

Toad catches my eye and actually goes red. He removes the hand which for some reason offends me, and steps away. "No, not today, and not ever again." His face goes stern as he passes the message on to them. "Go wait by the bar for me."

As the two girls walk away, with curious glances in my direction, he pulls me to one side. "Cilla and Easy live at the club. They, er, they take care of the brothers."

From the way they're dressed and the way they've come on to Toad, I don't need more information.

"You fuck them." My hands clench at my sides and my mouth twists with disgust.

A corner of Toad's mouth turns up. "So you can talk dirty, Princess? I like it." I want to wipe that grin off his face. He seems not to be stupid as his eyes flick between me and the girls who've just walked away. "Sure, I've fucked them. But," his hand touches my chin and raises my face until I'm forced to look at him, "from today, I'm off-limits, okay? You come to my bed, you'll be the only one there." I open my mouth, but he doesn't give me a chance. "And you want to sleep alone? Well, you'll be my ol' lady and I won't disrespect you that way. There's always my hand if you're not willing."

I'm angry, upset, and I'm not even sure why. If I don't want him, why should I worry if anyone else has him? "They're probably walking petri dishes," I snap.

"Princess, I always wear condoms and get tested regularly. I'm clean. And so, incidentally, are they. Brothers aren't stupid."

"Did you call them down so you could throw them in my face?"

He turns me around so I'm forced to look at them. The pair are standing at the bar, watching our altercation. "Look at them. Look at their faces."

I do. They're whores through and through, dressed in very little for one reason only, and their makeup is caked on. Though, as I look more carefully, I do see it's expertly applied.

"They can help you with your makeup. Disguise the bruises on your face." He pauses, swallows, and adds, half under his breath, "Fuck knows Easy had more than enough reason to learn how to do that before she came here."

I guess there's only one thing he's alluding to. "She was abused?"

"Every fuckin' day." Toad breathes out, his nostrils flaring. "And by her bastard of an ex."

I turn back to him. "And she puts up with you lot mauling her?"

"It took time," Toad confides. "Time for her to trust again. But she's safe here, and she knows it. She gets treated with respect. No consent, no play, Princess. Even for our club girls."

CHAPTER 9

TOAD

I didn't need Ruby to like me. All she had to do was go along with my plan to keep her safe. The club would get five million, and then I could carry on in the same way as I always have done. The only difference would be that I was married in name.

That was sight unseen. Once I'd met her, I knew I wouldn't kick her out of my bed, should she want to be in it. But if I'd harboured any thoughts about having her by my side as a true companion, and be in a relationship, well, that first meeting with her would have sealed it. We were so different we had about the same chance of gelling as oil and water.

But now she's here, in my world, and I'm watching her reactions.

While it would be a stretch to say she's relaxed, her nose isn't high in the air. She might have voiced a complaint, but as I walk her over to the bar and she catches sight of Rolo comfortably curled up in Raider's lap, instead, I catch a small smile which she quickly hides.

The clubhouse must be nothing like anything she's experienced, and me and my rough and admittedly vulgar brothers the type of people she'll never have met.

For a moment I wonder what I'd have done if I'd been dropped into her world. Like her, a complete fish out of water, I expect. On only my brief exposure to it, it had felt stifling. A servant for this, another for that. Even for one meal I'd felt like I'd been on show. Of course, my behaviour would have been regarded much like an animal in a zoo, and I couldn't give one fuck about it.

But Ruby's grown up with people watching her every move. Has she ever been able to relax? Somehow, I doubt it.

I watch her carefully as she approaches the club girls, waiting for that mask to rise. To my surprise, it doesn't. I open my mouth to speak for her, when again, astonishing me, she beats me to it.

"I'm Ruby," she introduces herself. "I was wondering whether you could help me. I'm marrying Toad in just over an hour, and," she points to her face, "I don't look particularly pretty."

Cilla's eyes go wide as she looks at me.

Wrapping my arm around my princess, I pull her close. "Can you help?"

"You're getting *married?*" Easy exclaims. "Goddamnit, Toad, why didn't we know already?"

"Well, you know now," I tell them. "Are you gonna help my bride?"

Cilla claps her hands. "Of course we are."

"Delivery, Toad!" Metalhead yells from behind me. He walks up, holding a couple of garment bags over his arm.

I take them from him, then do a small bow as I pass them to Ruby. "Your dress, ma'am."

"And this!" Raider comes over with a large box.

"They'll be my accessories," she states, offhandedly.

I expected to see a gleam in Ruby's eyes at the thought of getting dolled up in all her finery, but she takes them with a bored look on her face, peering in, then passing the smaller bag to me.

Guess she isn't excited about getting married to me. But then, why should she be? For the first time, I realise what a disappointment I am. She'd expected the fairy-tale wedding and the handsome prince, and instead, she got me.

I could tell her it's not forever.

But I'll be fucked. I want it to be. And ain't that a turn in the road I hadn't foreseen?

Cilla and Easy are good girls. Sure, they fight over biker cock, but won't much miss mine, as I seldom went with them. We'd rescued them both and given them a new chance in life. While they might have something to say in private about my soon-to-be wife, I doubt they'll insult her to her face.

So I stand back and let them take her away, then get Punchbag to hand me a shot.

"She's different to what I expected." Raider comes up beside me, tapping the bar and indicating he wants a beer. Punchbag obliges immediately.

After casting a quick glance behind him, satisfied when I find Rolo's now next to Cloud, I turn back. "She was different last night," I tell him. "When I said she was a stuck-up bitch, I meant it." Turning, I lean back against the bar and rest my elbows on it. "To be honest, Raid, I'm not sure what I feel about it."

"This marriage was going to be your finger to the rich," he sums up adequately. "You were going to show how they could be brought down to our level, to show what happens when they fuck up."

"Some deviant part of me wanted to corrupt her," I agree. "Brewster had no option except to come crawling to us, and you know how much I relished that."

Metalhead comes across to join us. I grin as I notice Rolo jumping up at his legs. Even at full height, her front paws don't reach his knees.

"I got the warning out to the other chapters," Metalhead states, as he plants his substantial ass on the bar stool, then leans down and scoops the little dog up. "When the time's right, we can make a united front against the cartel."

"And the time will be right in…" I take out my phone and glance at the screen, "about fifty-five minutes."

The clubroom door bursts open and in walk Cash, Beat

and Crumb. Apart from Stumpy, my enforcer, I think that's everyone here now. My treasurer's got a big grin on his face, and who can blame him?

He comes across. "My man." Cash slaps my back. "Five million's showing as pending on our fuckin' account."

"Let me see." Crumb pushes past him. "I ain't seen so many zeros before in my life."

Ignoring them, I motion for Punchbag to refill my glass, and slowly sip it. There's no doubt the money will come in handy and is the reason I'm making this sacrifice. So why do I suddenly feel like there's a bad taste in my mouth?

I shake off the feeling. My brothers deserve the windfall. Then, deciding I better get ready myself, I go upstairs to my room. Standing on the threshold, I check it's tidy, and that the prospects have done what I asked and made the bed up with fresh sheets. *And here I am, mocking her for having servants.* I snort. Slightly dubious, I open the bag she's handed me. She hasn't embellished my order. It's just a plain shirt, and a pair of black pants that look like they'll fit. I shower, change, shrug back into my cut, then I'm ready.

When I return downstairs, Metalhead wolf whistles at me, but I just show him my finger.

"We still having church later?" Raider asks.

"It's Friday, so yes." My brow furrows at the idea he'd think otherwise.

He grins wryly. "Thought you might have made other plans."

I hadn't. But now I come to think about it, getting hitched then returning straight to the clubhouse and disappearing for a meeting might not endear me to my new wife. But then, hell, she's got to learn to live with it. Plenty of time for us to get to know each other later.

"We'll make it short." The compromise comes out of my mouth before I realise I'm saying it.

"Don't fuckin' blame you, Prez. She's a looker." Bonk gets a slap around his head.

"Fuck it. That hurt, Prez. I was only saying the truth. Look."

I turn around and suck in air. By everything fuck-worthy, Ruby has scrubbed up alright. Her dress is classy, as I expected—a long satin sheath with a split up the side that goes to the top of her thigh. As she walks toward me, she flashes skin with each stride.

The club girls have done wonders with her makeup, and if I didn't know they were there, I doubt I'd be able to make out the shadow of bruises. Her hair is swept up in some kind of loose updo, that leaves curls covering the stitches.

How she can walk on those high heels I'll never know. They match her outfit perfectly—white, with diamanté sparkling with diamonds.

She looks like she's worth every penny that she spent of her dad's.

And she's mine. Or soon will be. My hands shake at the thought of it.

Another glance at my phone shows me she's exactly on time. As I approach her, she's biting her lip.

"Is it too much?" she asks.

"You're perfect." The only thing missing is that she's not wearing my property cut. I hadn't even thought about it. But now I realise the omission, I know it's not right, but it's far too late to do anything to rectify the matter.

I reach out my hand. "Shall we go do this then?"

"You've trimmed your beard."

I'm surprised she noticed. I just gave it a light tidy after my shower. I murmur non-committedly and continue walking her to the door. Once outside, I blink, then blink again, then roar with laughter.

"Which of you fuckers did this?"

Waiting for us is a fucking limousine. My princess giggles beside me.

"I take it you weren't expecting this?" she asks with mirth in her voice.

"No," I growl, looking around for the culprit.

"Well, whoever's responsible, thank you," Ruby calls out. Then her eyes narrow as I remove my cut. "You can wear that, you know. I, er, kinda like you in it."

Taken by surprise, I lean in closer. "I'll wear it for you later with nothing else if that's what you want." I pause at her sharp intake of breath, then add, "But for now it's disrespecting the patch if I wear my cut in a cage."

"Cut? Cage?" she questions.

Hell, she's got a lot to learn. "Car, cage. Leather vest, cut," I say simply, my attention caught by something else.

There's a fucking chauffeur who's patiently waiting, holding one of the back doors ajar. I allow her to slide in, then get in after her. Before the door shuts, Raider passes Rolo inside. Ruby takes a strand of red ribbon she's managed to find somewhere and ties a bow around the dog's neck.

I chuckle. "You've got a bridesmaid."

"Well, I'm not going to leave her out of it." Her smile fades. "Will… will my daddy be there?"

I take her hand and squeeze it. "No, darlin'." Grimacing, I add, "He's not supposed to know about it, remember?"

She takes a moment to process my words, and I'd have to be made of stone not to see how sad that makes her.

I reinforce my statement. "It's for your safety, and his."

She makes a grimace, then pulls back her shoulders. For a moment, we ride in silence. Then, showing she's no stranger to this mode of transport, she reaches forward, and slides shut the privacy glass between us and the driver. When she sits back, she turns to me, nervously.

"I'm not a virgin, you know."

My eyebrows rise. "You saying your daddy did some fake advertising?"

"I'm saying, Daddy doesn't know everything about his little girl." She fiddles nervously with her fingers. "Does that disappoint you?"

"Fuck no." I'm actually pleased. It means I won't have to hold back for fear of hurting her. "But I will say, you've only had boys before."

She chuckles. "That's what Easy and Cilla told me. Apparently, once I've experienced biker cock, I won't want anything else. That means you have a lot to live up to."

My brow furrows, and I turn sideways on the seat. "Princess, Ruby… Seriously. It's your decision what we do tonight. I'm not forcing you into anything. It's up to you, when, and if you're ready."

She stares at me earnestly, then her hand covers mine. "I know," she says softly. "I think you're a good man, Toad."

I suppress my snort. She doesn't know the half of it. "Does that mean you like me, just a little bit?"

She holds her thumb and forefinger a quarter of an inch apart. "Maybe a little bit."

Imitating her gesture, I reply to her, "Maybe I'm starting to like you too."

And I'll be fucked if we don't turn to each other and smile.

CHAPTER 10

RUBY

Every little girl dreams of their wedding day. They envision a beautiful dress carefully chosen, cake tasting, a reception arranged, and being given away by their father to the handsomest man in the world. Though the latter might be in their own eyes, of course.

Only one of those things I have today, the dress, but even that wasn't my choice but my shopper's. She knows my taste, the result is okay, but my opinion wasn't required.

It's elegant, stylish, but not the fairy-tale dress. But then, despite what Toad calls me, I'm no princess, this is no children's story, and Toad's not my handsome prince. I'd be crazy to think I'd have a happily ever after with a man I've only just met, and one I've absolutely nothing in common with.

My father won't even be there to give me away. This is far from the wedding of my dreams.

But what choice have I got? I can't even ask for a delay. Earlier, I was kidnapped by a man who thinks he has rights to me, a powerful man. Even I've heard of the cartel, and Enrico's name whispered quietly, in case just one mention would summon the man like the devil he is.

Since we've admitted we like each other, albeit only a small bit, and not much on which to base a real relationship, Toad's gone quiet, and I wonder whether he's thinking much the same way. He's as trapped as I am. Okay, so he's getting paid, but is the amount worth taking on the burden of me?

Maybe he's having similar doubts.

I hate the silence, so to break it, I ask, "What's your real name?" I'll hear it later, but it seems odd to be about to stand up to take my vows when the judge knows more about him than I do.

"Curtis McKenzie."

Ruby McKenzie. I try it on for size, deciding it has a nice ring to it.

"And Toad? Why do they call you that?"

He sighs, looks out of the window, then turns back to me. "Christ, Princess. You've just reminded me how old I am." His mouth twists. "When you must still have been in diapers, I joined the Navy, and then became a SEAL."

I sort of thought he was born into the MC and had done nothing else. "A SEAL?"

"A frogman." He chuckles quietly. "Road names aren't particularly inventive. Raider raids the fridge, Metalhead likes heavy metal."

"Bonk is bonkers and Scalpel a medic." I cotton on quickly. "But why Toad?"

"I prospected for the club while I was still in the service, well, at least I did while I was on leave. They called me Frog-man, Frog for short."

I give an unladylike snort. "You'd be my frog prince if you still had that name. But why did you change it?"

He points to the scar on his face, and his nose. "Because I became butt-ugly."

I realise I've become accustomed to his appearance. The scars and slightly crooked nose enhance him and in no way detract from his looks. His skin looks weatherworn, and to be honest, I prefer it from some of the fresh-faced boys I'd previously been with.

"You're not—" I start.

But instead of letting me finish, he takes a deep breath, then tugs his shirt out of his pants. Pulling it up, he turns his back to face me. "Full disclosure, Ruby."

I suck in air. His back, his poor, poor back. He goes to pull his shirt back down to cover his damaged skin, but I stop him, bunching the material up in my left hand while my hand traces the scarring. "What's this?"

"Bullet. Fuckin' sniper got me. A couple of inches to the left and he'd have killed me."

"And, this?" I run my hand over the puckered skin that covers his back from his neck and disappears beneath his waistband.

"IED. Basically, it was a firebomb and hit the hut we were sheltering in. I survived. I was lucky."

"You were burned," I say, unnecessarily, unable to process the pain he must have been in. "Skin grafts?"

"Yep." He chuckles, but there's no mirth in his tone. "I was lucky to be alive, others not so much. I was shipped stateside and somehow survived. Crawled back to the MC, more or less literally." Now he does chortle. "You know what sympathy those fuckers gave me? With the wounds still healing, my back looked even worse back then. They took one look at my back and immediately changed my name from that of a smooth-skinned frog to a wart-covered toad."

"That's so cruel." I cover my mouth with my hand.

"Nah." He pulls himself away, making me lose the grip on his shirt. When he tucks his shirt in again, he turns back to me. "It was what I needed, Princess. I was feeling sorry for myself. They gave me the necessary kick to pull my head out of my ass and accept how things had to be." He winks. "I was handsome back in the day."

He's still handsome now in a rugged way. It makes me put a different perspective on things. While I was, admittedly probably by then past the diaper stage, I was growing up without wanting for or worrying about anything. And there he'd been, brave, serving his country. He was lucky to escape with his life. Toad's not someone unworthy of me. He's seen and done things I can't begin to imagine.

I'm not marrying beneath my station today. In truth, I may be marrying beneath his.

What do I bring to this marriage but the wealth of my family when I haven't earned myself anything?

As the courthouse comes into sight, I take his hand. "You're my frog prince," I tell him, firmly.

"And you're my Princess," he whispers hoarsely back at me.

The limousine pulls to a halt. The chauffeur comes around and opens my door. I get out, then wait for Toad to come join me.

"Ready?" He raises an eyebrow as he asks.

I take a deep breath. "Toad, you needn't do this. You needn't save me."

"What?" His mouth quirks, as he adds in mock horror, "And lose my club five million dollars?"

But the twinkle in his eyes suggests this has become less about money, and more about something that's between him and me. The squeeze on my fingers, the gentle pressure of his hand in the small of my back, little things like that which aren't the actions of a man being forced to the altar.

When he slides on his cut, I swallow twice. Far from wondering whether this man is my equal, I start to question whether he sees anything in me.

We mount the steps into the building and are directed to the correct room. There, in front of the judge, in front of his MC as witnesses, with Raider, his best man by his side, and Rolo wagging her tiny tail at my feet, we prepare to commit ourselves to each other.

The judge stands up, and we stand before him. He coughs, opens his mouth, then the door to the room bursts open.

I spin around at the interruption, just as everyone else does.

It's Daddy.

He comes running up to me, his hands grabbing mine. His eyes look wild, but he looks happy.

"You shouldn't be here," I hiss, knowing he's put himself in danger.

He shakes his head, and announces loudly, "My beautiful girl. You don't need to do this."

"But I—"

Again, his head snaps right then left. "No, sweetheart. You don't. I've just heard. Enrico's dead. He was shot by border control when he tried to cross over. He's dead. You hear me? He's got no claim on you."

Enrico's dead? It's too much to process.

Casting my eyes toward my, up to this moment, husband-to-be, I see him stiffen. Daddy also notices.

"You'll get your money, Toad. You kept her safe. If it hadn't been for you, she'd have been kidnapped this morning, and once the cartel..." He doesn't finish. He doesn't have to, so he ends by lamely repeating, "You'll get your money."

There's stunned silence. Then it's Raider from his position at Toad's side who says, "Fuck the money, we want our princess."

Daddy splutters. "She's not your princess, she's my Ruby. Ruby, come on, you can come home now. Chef's making a special dinner to celebrate."

I can go back to a dinner, calorie counted and carefully nutritionally balanced, when I haven't even tasted what Dwarf can make. According to Easy, he makes a mean burger, and knows how to grill a spectacular steak.

Back to my maid and her expertise doing my hair when Cilla had done it to perfection earlier.

Back to the routine, back to the boring, back to the place where I have nothing to do and not much reason for my existence.

I turn to Toad. "This dog fighting ring stuff you have going on, your friend Snoop, do you think he needs help with the training and rehoming?"

Toad seems completely bewildered, both by my question

and the swift change in the proceedings. But I already have my answer. He'd already told me. *I can do anything.*

The confused judge has taken off his glasses and is swinging them on one finger. "Is this wedding going ahead or not?" he asks, impatiently.

"No," Toad and my father say together.

"Yes," I say firmly.

Toad turns to me fast, his face unreadable, but there's a glint in his eyes. "Princess…?"

"I want to marry you," I say shyly. "That's if you still want me."

Ignoring our audience, Toad steps closer. His hand snakes out, curling around my nape and holding me firmly. His mouth crashes down on mine and I immediately open for him. As his tongue invades, I have no impulse to push him away. As I breathe in his scent of leather, pine and oil, I make no move to step backward. Raising my hands, I pull his head down to mine, letting him know I don't want him to stop.

We've shared two other kisses, but this one is different. It's almost brutal in his claiming of me, and in return, I claim him back. Our tongues duel as I go on tiptoe, wanting even more pressure. My nipples peak as they rub against his cut, and I feel his engorged cock pressing against me.

It's sexy, it's animalistic, it's everything I ever wanted but never dared ask for.

When the clearing of a throat brings us to our senses, he gently pulls back, keeping our foreheads pressed together.

His gorgeous, sexy eyes stare into mine. "I want you, Ruby, like I've never wanted anything before." He raises his head, takes a deep breath, and for the first time I've seen, gives a genuine smile. "Ruby, Princess. Will you marry me?"

"Yes, my frog prince," I respond without hesitation.

"Ruby, this is crazy…"

I turn to my father, but before I can speak, a wizened

biker, who've I've not yet met, steps forward. He's as broad as he's tall, and only comes up to just above my shoulder.

"She said yes," he says gruffly. "She's ours now." Then he turns to me. "I'm Dwarf. Pleased to meetcha."

"Can we get on with this?" the judge snaps.

As Daddy steps back, outmanoeuvred and outnumbered, Toad and I resume our places in front of the judge. We both say our "I dos" and in front of the Wicked Warriors MC, and my father, we put rings on each other's fingers. I sign my new name in the register.

Ruby McKenzie.

Exiting the courthouse, the limousine drives to a park, and then stops, amidst a circle of motorbikes. It's there I get my Facebook and Instagram photos. Me, in my white dress, front and foremost. My prince in his cut by my side. Rolo in pride of place at my feet, the limousine, the symbol of my old life, behind us. All against the backdrop of bikers on their motor-cycles placed in a semi-circle, representing the start of a new chapter.

I'll post the pictures later.

As it turns out, much, much later. In the scheme of things, announcing my nuptials on social media doesn't seem as important as it once has.

CHAPTER 11

TOAD

The limousine ride back to the clubhouse is far too slow, too sedate for my liking. I can't wait to get Ruby on the back of my bike. I already know she belongs there.

When her dad had given her the perfect out, she'd chosen me. How the fuck did I get so lucky? How is it that I'm being driven home with a wedding ring on my finger?

And how, so quickly, does this feel so damn right?

Surely instalove only happens in fairy tales.

When we arrive at the clubhouse, I want to rush her inside, but instead, wait indulgently for Rolo to squat and do her business. Then, when she's finished, I grab Ruby's hand.

"Watch the dog!" I call out to Metalhead, as I rush her through the doorway.

"Hey, Prez, what about church?" Raider, the fucker, calls out.

"Fuck church," I call back. *I'm going to fuck my wife. That has to be better.*

There's the pop of a champagne bottle. *Where the fuck did that come from?*

"Prez, we're going to celebrate!" Bonk shouts.

"Celebrate without us." I pull Ruby, *my wife,* toward the stairs.

"Toad, slow down," she gets out through peals of laughter.

But fuck going slow. Noticing the problem she's having with her high heels, I sweep her into my arms.

"Looks like we'll celebrate later," she calls over my shoulder.

I take the stairs two at a time and kick my door open.

Then I set her down. I'm breathing heavily, not so much from exertion, as emotion.

She's mine, and I'm going to tell her. Fuck, I'm going to show her. But I sense the need to slow down, so gently I release her.

She looks up with her doe eyes, and if I wasn't there already, that's when I fall in love with her. She's gazing at me like I'm her saviour when there's no longer a need to save her.

I shudder as I take a breath. "I noticed your ass first." I palm said body area. "I think I fell in love right there."

"With my ass?" She snorts.

"Or when you turned round, and your shirt was plastered to your body with the rain, and your tits, well, it was a tossup between them and your ass."

"And what then?" she asks, batting her eyes, fishing for the next compliment.

"Woman, do you need to ask? It was your dog."

Her small hand forms a fist, and she goes to hit me, but I capture it, imprisoning it between us.

"I thought you were a total ass," she responds. "Rude, obnoxious. Then, you came to dinner."

"Then I came to dinner," I repeat, raising my brow.

She laughs. "You were so uncouth."

"I can be couth when I want to," I reassure her, grinning at the way I'd played her that night.

"I called you ugly. I didn't mean it."

"You did," I contradict her. And hell, why not. I'm not a pretty boy, and I've got the warts to prove it.

She grows serious, and whispers softly, "How's this going to work?"

"The princess and the biker?"

"Uh-huh." She rests her head against my chest as she waits for the answer.

"Well, I don't know, but I have a pretty good idea where

we can start. See, I've got a cock, you got a pussy, and I think we should see if they fit together."

"Toad," she says, her voice hoarse. "I never took you for much of a thinker, but I was wrong. I believe you're quite smart."

The dress she wore today, the way she stood up to her father, even how my club seem to have accepted her, have me more turned on than I can ever remember being. I might be in my mid-thirties, but right now I'm on a hair trigger, and worried my cock will fucking explode if she so much as touches me.

I never wanted a virgin princess. If I wanted anyone, it would be a woman who could handle me. I couldn't be happier that she's experienced and I'm not the least concerned mine won't be the first cock to touch her.

The need for conversation has passed. I'm all for action. I crowd her, knowing the expression on my face is one of desperate hunger. She doesn't back away from me, instead, a corner of her mouth curls as if she knows the power she holds.

"I'm going to take that dress off you." That's the only warning I give before I slide my knife out of its sheath and, pulling the material away from her body, start slicing down from the cleavage, angling the line of my cut so it meets the slitted opening on her thigh. Like a banana emerging from its skin, she's quickly revealed to me.

Another woman might remind me how much the dress cost, or how she wanted to keep it as a reminder of our wedding day, but not my princess. This was no normal wedding. My ring might be on her finger but that means little to me until I've taken her, marked her and claimed her.

Her shopper had done excellently. She's wearing a white satin bra and matching panties. I slice through the bra, then putting my knife away, place both hands at her hips, pull, tear, and her probably very expensive panties fall away. All she's now wearing are those fuck-me shoes.

She's smooth and bare, exactly how I like my women to be. My nostrils twitch as the aroma of her arousal reaches me.

"Are you wet for me, Princess?"

She gives a shy nod of her head, and swallows. I could ask her to prove it to me, but I decide to check for myself. With one arm circling her waist, I gently circle the fingers of my other hand first on her stomach, then inch them lower, feeling her muscles quiver beneath me.

As I home in on my target, her breath hitches.

When I reach her clit, toying with it for just one moment, she jolts.

When I slide my fingers through the copious moisture leaking from her slit and can't resist raising my hand to my lips to taste her, she moans my name loudly.

Fuck, she tastes sweet.

My own breathing unsteady, I sink to my knees, tapping her legs until she widens them for me. Then I put my face in her crotch, inhaling deeply. She smells of all my favourite seasons rolled into one, a hint of the soap she uses, and something uniquely her. It's that moment I realise, I've been supping on cheap wine previously. Now I'm going to dine like a king.

My notion confirmed as I place my mouth there, her flavour hitting my tastebuds for the first time. It's like sampling champagne and proves just as heady as I lap at her cream.

Her hands tangle in my hair, gripping it tight as though to keep herself steady as I go to work, piercing her slit with my tongue, then using it to circle her clit, while pushing my fingers into her tight sheath.

Her pussy seems to be trying to suck my digits in, and my cock hardens to the point it's painful. My balls throb as her taste, the feel of her, the sounds that she's making, and even the sting of her hands as they pull at my hair, combine to ramp up my arousal.

I nibble, suck, circle my tongue around her clit, rewarded by her muscles clenching and a cry coming out of her mouth. When I curl up my fingers inside her, finding that spot that feels spongy and press on it, she yells out my name and convulses around me.

Her muscles spasm, and I feel her stagger. My free hand locks on her hips to give her the support she needs. Then, when her tension begins to ease, I stand, pull her into my arms, and plant my mouth on hers.

There's no objection, she's tasting herself as my tongue pushes its way between her lips. She clutches at me as if I'm her lifeline.

Gently, I pull back, planting a chaste kiss to the side of her mouth. "Fuck, I need you."

"I'm yours."

She sure is. *Mine.* As if my cock needed more encouragement, it jerks, reminding me it wants in on the action.

"Lie down," I manage to spit out, my tone scratchy and an octave lower than normal. I'm proud that I'm able to form words.

Sex is a function, a physical release to relieve tension. That's the way I've always approached it before. Whether it's been by my hand, or in a pussy, the effect has meant nothing more than a way to let loose, preserve my sanity and prevent blue balls.

With her, I already know it's going to be different. She's erased all memories of other pussy, exceeded every one and spoiling me for the future. But what do I care? She's mine, as somehow, she was always destined to be.

Now she's lying on my bed like she's meant to be there. Her gorgeous blue eyes fixated on me as I remove my cut and reverently place it over the back of a chair. Her hands flutter as though in encouragement as I take hold of each side of my shirt and tear. Buttons fly off in all directions as her chin raises slightly in total agreement. There's no time for delay or a tantalising striptease.

She doesn't need it. She just needs me.

I toe off my boots. They crash and rumble as they slide across the floor. Then she licks her lips in anticipation as I unfasten my belt, flick open the button, then lower the zip. Continuing in one smooth movement, I slide down the pants she'd given me earlier.

I've gone commando just for this moment and am rewarded as she swallows hard when my cock leaps free.

Then I'm naked, crawling over the bed to get to her.

"I'm on the pill," she tells me, her tongue moving over her lips again.

I've never trusted a woman before, but I trust her. In the back of my mind, there's even the thought that if she's lying, I wouldn't care. "I'm clean," I manage to rasp out.

I'm going to take her bare.

It's not just my dick that's hard. Every part of me is tense, so desperate to get inside her. But then my eyes fall on the imperfections marring her perfect skin, the black-and-blue evidence of bruising on her ribs.

With rigid control, I trace the bruising with a gentle touch. "Do these hurt?"

"What hurts?" Her voice is breathless. "I don't care, Toad. Just take me now."

"I'll try to be gentle." Though fuck knows how.

"I don't want gentle. I want my biker."

I need no further encouragement. In one swift move, I have her legs open and her ankles up over my shoulders, grinning a little at her surprised gasp as I tug her hips up. Then, lining myself up, I push forward.

Fuck, she's tight. I try to fight my baser instincts to simply surge up inside her.

"Fuck me, Toad." She presses her hands into the mattress

and tries to push down on me and moves her hips to encourage me inside.

Oh fuck. Whatever semblance of control I had, I lose. I thrust deep as I invade her snug channel, feeling it fitting me like a glove. I pause, my eyes crossing, as I simply relish the feeling of being in her.

"Fuck me already," she whines, trying to get me moving.

She's my princess, but she's not holding back. It seems in bed, we're going to be more than compatible. And I'm her prince. What choice have I got but to obey her?

"Get ready," I warn her.

I get down to business. I roll my hips, thrust up into her, calling on every move in my repertoire, noting her reaction when I hit her G-spot.

Her head is thrown back, her chest heaving. Her hands grip at the sheets, and her mouth opens wide. Her whole body flushes as blood rushes to the extremities.

I try to hold back, but she uses her Kegels, pulsating down on my cock as if purposefully trying my limits.

Never, before her, have I had to distract myself by thoughts of the number of bolts on my bike to delay doing the unthinkable and coming prior to her.

At last, her body tenses. She gasps and stops breathing.

I thought I'd known pleasure before. I thought I'd experienced everything. But when she clamps down on my dick and my name comes from her mouth when she comes around me, I know I've only lived in black and white before. Now, I'm able to see in colour.

I roar, me, who's always orgasmed quietly. I fucking roar out my completion. Sex has never been like this previously.

When my balls are emptied completely, I open my eyes which had, of their own volition, squeezed shut, to find her smiling at me.

"Fuck, Princess. My Ruby." Overcome with emotion, I can barely form words. "Fuck, you were made for me."

"My prince," she responds, her own voice choking. "I'm yours."

"Mine," I repeat.

We gaze at each other silently.

A silence broken by a light scrabbling at the door.

"No, Rolo. C'mere. Mommy and Daddy are busy," Raider's voice sounds.

I quirk an eyebrow at her. "You're never going to be calling me Daddy."

She laughs, the action pushing my now depleted cock from her body. Ignoring the mess, I pull her to me, holding her gently, well aware of her sore ribs. Her mirth is infectious, and I, too, start laughing.

"It all started with Rolo," she tells me.

"No, Princess, it started long before. I think we were destined to be together from your birth."

There's no other explanation for it. She's perfect for me, and hopefully, I for her.

It's not often I'm sappy, but when I whisper into her ear, "Our happily ever after starts right now," I mean it.

"If I'm your princess, then I think I've found my prince," she whispers back.

Thanks for reading! Please add a short review on Warts n' All and let me know what you thought!

DANI AND THE OUTCAST by R.E. Hargrave

Bleeding Souls Saved by Love! A Fabled Retelling of LADY AND THE TRAMP

~

Once upon a time, a Louisiana mafia princess grew up in privilege. In her world, no one went hungry, status mattered, and life moved along like a fairytale. And just like in a fairytale, the princess longed for something more than being handed everything on a silver platter… or, at the hilt of a .38 Colt.

~

PROLOGUE

All around existed a flurry of activity which kept eyes off him. Mixers, bowls, and baking stones pulled from the kitchen cupboard left him an open space to hide. It was his usual spot; of course, his lanky twelve-year-old body barely fit these days. They all knew he was there but entertained him nonetheless with their faux curiosity of "where could the boy be."

The game continued until his mother appeared. If anyone denied the knowledge of his whereabouts, Madame Rossi would have their job, if not their head. His kitchen friends didn't deserve her ire over his antics, and so, at the anger in her voice, he crawled from the space.

Seeing the emotions pass through her eyes before she settled on frustration raised his own.

How dare they take my father. How dare they do this to my mother.

"*Stai scherzando*, Vincenzo! Why aren't you dressed yet? We leave for the church in fifteen minutes. Run, boy. Run."

"Si, Mamma," he replied and scurried off. Once he was out of her sight, the thought of the stupid suit waiting for him slowed his pace.

He'd had to wear the thing less than a month ago to bury his father. Donning it again would not equal celebration, and he could care less about his aunt's wedding. All he wanted was for everyone to clear out of his villa to let him and his mother grieve. The villa was *his* now. His father, the King of the Rossi Famiglia, had told him only a few months ago prior that, in the event of his death, *he* would become the man of the house… and leader of the Famiglia. Leonardo Rossi had been shrewd, cunning, and preparing Vincenzo for his future role from the moment the boy could speak. That'd he'd been given such warnings so early in his life spoke volumes on his father's distrust of people within the organization.

What he'd learned since the funeral threw a wrench in his father's plan, *his* plan, and confirmed the man had been right to groom his son. Not for one second did Vincenzo believe the awful lies they were telling about his father. There was no way Leonardo had betrayed Famiglia. He most certainly had not deserved to die such a brutal death at the hands of Chicago's soldiers.

It had been a closed casket service due to the damage, and the number of pieces, the former King had been found in.

Louisiana belonged to the Italians, not those "damn, pasty Frenchmen," as his father always called them. Vincenzo was too young to do anything about it now, but one day, he vowed, he would get his revenge, and reclaim the Rossi family honor.

Releasing January 15, 2022

https://books2read.com/DaniAndTheOutcast

ABOUT THE AUTHOR

Manda Mellett is the creator of the popular Satan's Devils MC. A series that currently has twenty-nine books including the original Arizona Chapter and four spin-off chapters. She's experienced her own instalove with her bike-riding husband which so far has lasted 34 years.

Newsletter

Stalk, Love, And Share The Authors!

Alexi Ferreira
Facebook
Instagram
Twitter
Bookbub
Goodreads
Amazon
Newsletter

P.T. Macias
Facebook
Instagram
Twitter
Bookbub
Goodreads
Amazon
Newsletter

Nicole Banks
Facebook
Instagram
Bookbub
Goodreads
Amazon

Rowan St. George
Facebook
Instagram
Twitter
Bookbub
Goodreads
Amazon

N.J. Adel
Facebook
Instagram
Twitter
Bookbub
Goodreads
Amazon
Newsletter

Linzi Basset
Facebook
Instagram
Twitter
Bookbub
Goodreads
Amazon
Newsletter

Sahara Roberts
Facebook
Instagram
Twitter
Bookbub
Goodreads
Amazon
Newsletter

LM Mountford
Facebook
Instagram
Twitter
Bookbub
Goodreads
Amazon
Newsletter

Reagan Phillips
Facebook
Instagram
Twitter
Bookbub
Goodreads
Amazon
Newsletter

Jessica Joy
Facebook
Instagram
Twitter
Bookbub
Goodreads
Amazon

JA Lafrance
Facebook
Instagram
Twitter
Bookbub
Goodreads
Amazon
Newsletter

Felicity Brandon
Facebook
Twitter
Bookbub
Goodreads
Amazon
Newsletter

Jessica Avary

Facebook
Instagram
Twitter
Bookbub
Goodreads
Amazon

Leah Negron
Facebook
Instagram
Twitter
Bookbub
Goodreads
Amazon
Newsletter

Cedar Rose
Facebook
Instagram
Bookbub
Goodreads
Amazon

Honey Palomino
Facebook
Instagram
Twitter
Bookbub
Goodreads
Amazon

Michelle Corchis
Facebook
Instagram
Bookbub

Goodreads
Amazon

MD Stewart
Facebook
Instagram
Bookbub
Goodreads
Amazon

Candi Fox
Facebook
Instagram
Twitter
Bookbub
Goodreads
Amazon

K R Hall
Facebook
Instagram
Twitter
Bookbub
Goodreads
Amazon

Sofia Aves
Facebook
Instagram
Twitter
Bookbub
Goodreads
Amazon

Kaci Rose

Facebook
Instagram
Twitter
Bookbub
Goodreads
Amazon

Ember-Raine Winters
Facebook
Instagram
Twitter
Bookbub
Goodreads
Amazon

L.D. Wosar
Facebook
Instagram
Twitter
Bookbub
Goodreads
Amazon

Louisa Bacio
Facebook
Instagram
Twitter
Bookbub
Goodreads
Amazon

Andrea Marie
Facebook
Instagram
Bookbub

Stalk, Love, And Share The Authors!

Goodreads
Amazon

Jenna Gunn
Facebook
Instagram
Twitter
Bookbub
Goodreads
Amazon

Gillian Grey
Facebook
Amazon

R.E. Hargrave
Facebook
Instagram
Twitter
Bookbub
Goodreads
Amazon

OTHER WORKS BY MANDA MELLETT

<u>*Blood Brothers – A series about sexy dominant sheikhs and their bodyguards*</u>

Stolen Lives (#1) Nijad and Cara

Close Protection (#2) Jon and Mia

Second Chances (#3) Kadar and Zoe

Identity Crisis (#4) Sean and Vanessa

Dark Horses (#5) Jasim and Janna

Hard Choices (#6) Aiza

Satan's Devils MC - Arizona Chapter

Turning Wheels (Blood Brothers #3.5, Satan's Devils #1) Wraith and Sophie

Drummer's Beat (#2) Drummer and Sam

Slick Running (#3) Slick and Ella

Targeting Dart (#4) Dart and Alex

Heart Broken (#5) Heart and Marc

Peg's Stand (#6) Peg and Darcy

Rock Bottom (#7) Rock and Becca

Joker's Fool (#8) Joker and Lady

Mouse Trapped (#9) Mouse and Mariana

Blade's Edge (#10) Blade and Tash

Heart Mended: A Satan's Devils MC Novella

Truck Stopped (#11) Truck & Allie

Satan's Devils MC Boxset 1 Books 1-5

Satan's Devils MC Boxset 2 Books 6-8

Satan's Devils MC Boxset 3 Books 9-11

Satan's Devils MC - Colorado Chapter

Paladin's Hell (#1) Paladin and Jayden

Demon's Angel (#2) Demon and Violet

Devil's Due (#3) Beef and Steph

Devil's Dilemma (#4) Pyro and Mel

Ink's Devil (#5) Ink and Beth

Devil's Spawn (#6)

Satan's Devils MC - Next Generation

Amy's Santa (#1) Wizard and Amy

Hawk's Cry (#2) Hawk and Olivia

Twisted Throttle (#3) Throttle and Gwen

Satan's Devils MC - San Diego Chapter

Being Lost (#1)

Grumbler's Ride (#2)

Avenging Devil Part 1 (#3)

Avenging Devil Part 2 (#4)

Satan's Devils MC - Utah Chapter

Road Tripped (#1)

Stormy's Thunder (#2)

Satan's Devils MC - Las Vegas Chapter

Red's Peril - Part 1

Red's Peril - Part 2

www.ingramcontent.com/pod-product-compliance
Lightning Source LLC
Chambersburg PA
CBHW070447170726
48291CB00005B/1636